Polar Melt

A Novel

Martin Roy Hill

32-32 North

San Diego, CA

POLAR MELT

Copyright © 2018 by Martin Roy Hill

Published by

32-32 North

San Diego, CA

An imprint of
M. R. Hill Publishing
San Diego, California

ISBN: 0692096469
ISBN-13: 978-0692096468
For information contact:
www.martinroyhill.com

Cover Image: Tenedos | DepositPhotos.com

Cover Design: RebecaCovers

Books by Martin Roy Hill

Duty: Stories of Mystery and Suspense from the Cold
War and Beyond (2012)

The Killing Depths (2012)

Empty Places (2013)

Eden: A Sci-Fi Novella (2014)

The Last Refuge (2016)

The Butcher's Bill (2017)

War Stories (2018)

To the men and women of the United States Coast Guard—active, reserve, and auxiliary. The first branch of the military I served in, and my favorite.

Semper Paratus

Chapter 1

T here it is!"
The crewman pointed off the port quarter of the Research Vessel Franklin where a small, yellow object bobbed among the scattered floes of Arctic ice. The ship's captain and the team's chief research scientist stood together on the port wing of the bridge and waited for the hatch on the small submarine to open.

Officially referred to as a deep submergence vehicle, or DSV, the mini-sub was launched nearly a day before to explore beneath the disappearing Arctic ice. It was summer in the Arctic, and the once-permanent ice cap was at its lowest ebb in recorded history. The massive ice flows that usually choked the so-called Northwest Passage were little more than over-sized ice cubes floating in an empty sea thanks to warming global temperatures. The Franklin, a research vessel built by the U.S. Navy and operated under charter by a renowned oceanographic institute, had been researching—with the help of its DSV—the impact of so much melted fresh water on the native saltwater species that lived in the frigid Arctic Ocean.

Several hours into its mission, communication with the sub was lost. Though concerned, the Franklin's crew wasn't alarmed at first. Communications failures were routine. Plus, the DSV was the latest design and had the ability to make its own air. Still, a wave of relief swept through the crew at the sight of the mini-sub. Relief soon gave way to apprehension when the DSV's access hatch didn't open.

"What are they waiting for?" asked the captain. "You'd expect them to pop the hatch as fast as possible."

"Maybe they had an accident," said the scientist. "Maybe they're injured and can't turn the dogging wheel."

The captain nodded, cupped his hands to his mouth, and hollered to the crew members on the fantail. "Away all divers!"

A small, orange Zodiac launch sped away from the side of the ship and toward the DSV. Aboard was a coxswain to drive the boat and three divers in cold-water dry suits to re-trieve the sub. Within minutes, they were alongside the DSV and a diver clambered on board. He tried to open the hatch. The dogging wheel wouldn't turn. He took a knife from a sheath on his belt and used the hilt to bang a signal on the hull of the sub. There was no response.

The diver looked at the coxswain and shook his head. The coxswain picked up the radio mic and said, "Access hatch won't open, skipper. And we get no response from in-side."

"Bring her on in—fast," the captain said into his handheld radio.

Within fifteen minutes the DSV bobbed at the Frank-lin's stern, where the ship's massive A-frame crane waited to lift it on board. The divers attached the crane's cables to the sub's lifting points, and the crane's operator eased it from the water and into its cradle on the ship's stern deck.

The ship's chief bosun was ready with a dogging wrench. He climbed aboard the submarine, jammed the wrench between the spokes of the dogging wheel, and pulled. The muscles in his arms corded with strain.

Finally, it turned.

With a hiss, the hatch cracked open and the bosun peered in. The ship's medic bounded onto the sub and looked into the hatch. They straightened, looked at each other a moment, faces ashen, then the bosun turned to the crew on the deck.

"It's empty," he said.

Chapter 2

T he U.S. Navy MH-53E Sea Dragon roared across the north Alaska coastline, its three five-thousand horse-power engines deafening the six passengers on board. For this mission, the Sea Dragon carried only the pilot, co-pilot, and crew chief as crew. Six passengers huddled in the rear cabin, checking their equipment, reading, or sleeping. They wore battle gear—dark-blue trousers and blouse, and matching foul-weather jacket. Black gloves covered their hands, and black balaclavas concealed most of their faces. Black load-bearing ballistic armor vests protected their tor-sos. Each wore a Kevlar helmet of the same color, along with ballistic goggles. Each person had a Glock pistol either in a thigh-rigged holster or in a holster on their vest. Five carried M4 carbines with optical scopes; the sixth carried a M249 Squad Automatic Weapon, also known as a SAW machine gun, with a heavy box magazine. None wore any sign of rank or branch of service on their heavy jackets or vests.

Only twenty-four hours before, the helicopter crew re-ceived orders to deliver this group to a specific longitude and latitude in the Arctic Ocean. There was no doubt the Sea Dragon, with its long-range and air-refueling capability, could fly the distance. However, when the pilot plotted the location on his air chart, he complained there was nothing there but open ocean. "There's something there now," he was told, and nothing more. Nor did the passengers offer any more information.

His curiosity piqued, the crew chief duck-walked over to the one who appeared in charge and held his mouth next to the other's ear.

"Who are you guys, anyway?" he asked.

"U. S. Coast Guard," the man answered.

"Bullshit," said the crew chief. "Coast Guard way out here, armed like you? You guys must be CIA. You're CIA, aren't you?"

"Fine," the man said. "We're CIA."

The crew chief smiled and nodded, his suspicion confirmed. Then the nodding stopped, and the smile vanished.

"Wait a minute," he said. "If you were CIA, you wouldn't admit it."

"Maybe that's why I told you we were Coast Guard."

The man sitting next to the first man tapped his shoulder and pointed out a window. The coastline beneath them writhed with thousands of rotund, dark-brown bodies.

"Sea lions," the second man said.

From the uncovered skin around the second man's eyes, the crew chief could tell he was African American. And he wore black horned-rimmed glasses, which the Navy man thought odd. He'd never seen a spook or other special operator wearing glasses.

"Why are they crowded up like that?" asked the first man.

"The polar melt, sir," the black man said. "Normally, they would swim around the large ice floes looking for food or resting on the ice. Because of polar melt, they have nowhere else to go except the shoreline."

He gestured toward the ocean below. It was summer in the northern latitudes, and the Arctic's Chukchi Sea was still white with a thin layer of drift ice. Missing, however, was the thick pack ice, which only a few years before covered the Arctic Ocean even in summer.

The African American shook his head. The other man did the same. Strange conversation for spooks, the crew chief thought, and he moved forward toward the cockpit.

Sometime later, the crew chief came back and found the leader asleep. He shook him awake, careful not to stand too close to him. These special ops guys, he knew, didn't appreciate being roused from their sleep. The man opened his eyes and the crew chief hooked a thumb over his shoulder.

"Pilot wants to talk to you," he said.

The team leader nodded, stood, and made his way forward, stumbling once or twice from the bucking of the aircraft. When he entered the cockpit, the pilot in the right-hand seat pointed to an object below them.

"That your ship?"

Below them a ship wallowed in the ice-speckled ocean. She had a dark-blue hull and white superstructure. At the aft end of the superstructure stood a large white globe housing the antennae for the HiSeasNet oceanographic telecommunications system. On the stern was a large A-frame crane and, sitting in a cradle beneath it, a small submarine. The sub's cradle sat on a railroad-like track leading into a hanger. Forward of the bridge on the second, or O-2, deck, was a small helipad, marked with a large H within a circle.

The leader studied the vessel, comparing it to the photos he'd memorized during his mission briefing, and nodded.

"That's it," he said.

"That helipad is too small for us to put down on," said the pilot.

"Understood," the leader said. "We came prepared for that. Just put us over the flight deck and we'll fast rope."

"Roger that," answered the pilot.

Back in the cabin, the leader signaled his team. They stood and turned to a large duffel bag they had been leaning against. From inside the duffel, they removed a large coil of thick, braided nylon rope with an eye spliced into one end. Whipping secured the other end from fraying. They secured the eye into the maw of a hook above their heads and waited.

As they approached the vessel, the crew chief opened the aircraft's belly hatch and, secured by a safety harness, leaned out. The chilled Arctic wind swept through the cabin, and everyone shivered with the sudden onslaught. Guided by the crew chief, the pilot settled the giant helicopter in a hover over the ship's helo pad. The crew chief stood and motioned the team leader toward the hatch.

"Time to go," he said, though no one heard him.

The team leader picked up the coil of rope and tossed it out the hatch. The first one out the door was the man with the SAW machine gun. Then went the team leader, followed by another. Then smallest team member waddled to the door, burdened by heavy gear. The team member glanced at the crew chief with feminine eyes, winked once, then grabbed the rope and slid away.

My god, was that a woman?

The penultimate team member followed, with the black team member going last. When the entire team was on the ship's landing pad, the crew chief unhooked the rope and let it fall. He made his way toward to the cockpit.

The Sea Dragon was moving away from the ship when the crew chief poked his head into the cockpit, shaking his head.

"What is it?" asked the pilot.

"I could have sworn one of those guys was a girl," he said.

"Don't be ridiculous," the pilot said. He took the helicopter to altitude and turned it toward the mainland. "What do you think? You really believe what that guy told you? That they're Coast Guard?"

The crew chief pondered the question, then shook his head.

"Nah," he said. "What the hell would the Shallow Water Navy be doing way out here?"

Chapter 3

C oast Guard Lieutenant Commander Douglas Munro Gates, landed on the helo deck of the Research Vessel Franklin, stepped away from the rope, and dropped to one knee, his M4 at the ready. The first team member to land on the ship, Gunner's Mate 1st Class Jess Brown, kneeled to Gates' left, his SAW machine gun at his shoulder. As each member arrived, they, too, took up a position in a circular perimeter beneath the helicopter.

When the helo moved off, Gates signaled his team to move out. As one, the team rose and, weapons shouldered, spread out, scanning the vessel's small helipad and the foredeck below. There was nothing to see. At another hand signal from Gates, the team broke off into twos and headed to their designated search areas. Gates and his executive officer, Lieutenant (junior grade) Leland Strange, the man the Navy crew chief identified as African American, climbed toward the bridge, searching compartments along the way. Brown joined the team's engineering specialist, Senior Chief George Hopper, and headed for main engineering. Chief Georgia Stalk, the team's electronics expert, and Frank Chee, a 1st class aviation survival specialist and the team's medic, made for the research vessel's science center and its elaborate mix of ocean sensors and laboratories. Each team took a prearranged, circuitous route to their destinations that allowed them to search most of the ship's compartments along the way.

Together, these sailors made up the Coast Guard's Deployable Specialized Force–P. Deployable Specialized Forces, or DSFs, included units designed for anti-terrorism response, counter-insurgency warfare, coastal and riverine warfare, long-range drug interdiction, and chemical response. Of these, DSF–Papa was the smallest, most specialized, and least known, even within the Coast Guard itself. Those who did know of its existence insisted the P stood for Phenomena, since the team's mission was to investigate mysterious occurrences at sea that could endanger international maritime trade.

Such an occurrence involved the R/V Franklin. Five days before, the mainland lost all communications with the ship, including the vessel's AIS, or Automatic Identification System, a satellite identifier beacon that tracked vessels across the world's oceans. For five days, Coast Guard and Navy C-130 aircraft had flown missions over the Franklin's last known position, flying search patterns that accounted for the set and drift of the ocean that could have carried the ship or debris one direction or another. Hampered by fog, the searchers found no trace of the ship.

Then, twenty-four hours earlier, as the Coast Guard was about to list the ship as presumed sunk, one of its planes spotted the Franklin. The aircrew hailed the ship by radio and signal lamp, with no response. The gravity davits for the ship's lone lifeboat stood empty, and from what the flight crew could see, the ship was abandoned. The photographs they brought back convinced their superiors of the same. DSF–Papa deployed to investigate what the news media were already describing as a ghost ship.

Gates and Strange reached the bridge without any sign of crew members. The pilothouse, though crammed with electronic monitors and instruments, was otherwise empty.

The wheel stood locked with rudders amidships and the engine controls were in the all-stop position. Electronic screens, bridge radio, global positioning satellite monitor, and radar console were all lifeless. Gates punched the power button on each piece of equipment, and each remained cold and dead.

The cramped chart room aft of the bridge was lifeless as well, as was the tiny deep submergence vehicle observation lab behind it. The lower compartments they checked on the way to the bridge—the ship's sickbay, and officers' and scientists' staterooms—were also deserted.

Gates' radio earphone squelched and he heard Hopper's voice say, "Hopper to Gates, over."

"Gates. Go."

"Engineering spaces are secured, sir," Hopper said. "Secured, crewless, and without power. Over."

"Roger," replied Gates. "Same for all compartments above the O-2 deck. Over."

Aboard ships, decks above the main deck up are numbered in sequence O-1, O-2, O-3 and so forth. Decks below the main deck, called the lower decks, were simply numbered second, third, and so on the lower they went.

The Franklin had five upper decks, and three lower decks. The O-1 housed the conference room/library, the galley and mess deck, berthing for the crew, and an electrical shop. The next deck up, the O-2, housed sickbay and more crew berthing, while the O-3 held the staterooms for the senior scientists and officers. The O-4 deck, where the two officers stood, held the bridge, chart room, and DSV lab. The small O-5 deck above that was the fly bridge, where a lookout could get a more distant view of the horizon. Science labs filled the main deck compartments, while the second and third decks held engineering spaces and store rooms.

Gates heard more squelch, and Chief Stalk said, "Break. Stalk to Gates. Main and second deck compartments secured and just as empty. Over."

"Where the hell is everyone?" Gates muttered. Then he thumbed the push to talk button on his radio and said, "Roger. Double-check everything again. We'll meet in the ship's conference room in . . ." Gates checked his watch. "In fifteen mikes. Gates out."

Gates removed his Kevlar helmet and balaclava and ran his hand through straight, black hair cut short. His handsome face was long and narrow, its dark complexion darkened more by the sun and beginning to form creases around the dark-brown eyes and the thin, determined lips. He pulled an encrypted satellite telephone from a large pouch on his vest and turned it on.

"Leland, find the logbook and see if you can glean anything from it. I'm going out on the bridge wing and try to get a sat phone signal."

Strange took off his K–Pot and glasses, pulled the balaclava over his head, and scratched his short, curly, black hair.

"Aye, sir," he said, then disappeared into the chart room.

The Franklin's conference room was a much nicer meeting place than seen on Coast Guard cutters. A long buff-topped table, bolted to the deck, stretched across the center of the room, surrounded by no-nonsense, gray metal chairs. The chairs stood on sturdy metal legs with no wheels that would let them roll in a heavy sea. A well-padded love seat and matching lounge chairs lined the bulkheads, along with shelves crowded with scientific reference books. In one corner stood a smaller bookcase filled with novels of various genres, their spines creased and pages well-worn and dogged-eared.

"Lieutenant Strange, did you find the ship's log?" asked Gates.

The entire team sat around the meeting table, except for Chee, who stood watch as bridge lookout.

"The finished log is missing, sir," Strange said. "I found the rough log stuck between the chart table and a filing cabinet. It looks like it fell there."

Aboard ship, the events of each day are hastily recorded as they occur in a rough log. Later, that log is rewritten for clarity in what is known as the finished log.

"Anything of interest?"

"Not that we don't already know, sir," Strange said, adjusting his horn-rims.

Strange had boyish good looks, a face that to many looked too young for a Coast Guard officer. Still, the heavy black horn-rimmed glasses made him look very professorial, which, in fact, he was.

"It recorded the Franklin launched its DSV at 0900 hours seven days ago with an operator and two scientists," Strange continued. "After several hours of diving, the Franklin experienced severe interference on their Gertrude—"

The lieutenant looked up and explained, "That's the device they use to communicate with the DSV."

"Yes, sir," Chief Stalk said, a faint southern drawl in her voice. She was in her late thirties, with a stockiness that came from muscle not fat. She wore no makeup, but her large, green eyes and naturally long lashes made it appear as though she did. The eyes could scare a man or make him fall in love with her. It didn't matter to Stalk. After a bad divorce, her only current love was the service and the opportunity it afforded her to play with some of the most advanced electronic technology. "Gertrude is a nickname for the UQC, AN/WQC-2 underwater telephone used for underwater comms since 1945."

"Right," said Strange, stretching out the word. "Anyway, after the interference on Gertrude, Franklin lost contact with the sub. This particular DSV is of a very advanced design, capable of generating its own oxygen. The Franklin was not too worried at first. They just remained on station, trying to reestablish comms with it and notified Anchorage of the missing DSV. On the second day, the DSV surfaced, missing its crew. That was the last entry."

Gates nodded.

"That's what their last radio message was to Coast Guard Sector Anchorage," he said. "Then radio comms with Franklin was lost, along with its AIS signal."

Gates thought for a moment.

"So, whatever happened to the Franklin to make it disappear and the crew to abandon it had to happen shortly after they found the DSV," he said. "A short enough time so nothing else of note occurred that would have been recorded in the logbook."

"Or they were unable to write anything more in the log, sir," said Hopper. "Perhaps they were incapacitated someway."

Gates nodded.

"I find the symmetry of this situation quite interesting," the lieutenant said.

"Symmetry?" Gates raised his eyebrows.

"Yes, sir." Strange steepled his fingers in front of his face. "A ship disappearing at sea is not unusual. After all, it's a big ocean. It happens all the time. Perhaps at some point, that ship is discovered wrecked ashore or sunk or maybe even still afloat. What happened to it is a singular mystery. But here we have a mystery within a mystery. First, the DSV disappears, then reappears without its crew. Then the Franklin itself disappears and turns up without *its* crew. The two disappearances and reappearances are too similar to be natural or accidental."

"You're saying not only the disappearances are related, there was an external causal factor involved," Gates said.

"Yes, sir," said Strange.

Senior Chief Hopper grunted. In his forties, he had a half-ring of dwindling, gray hair sheared so tight to the scalp he appeared to be totally bald. By contrast, his regulation mustache looked bushy. He had dark, sardonic eyes. Somewhere he had found an empty soda can, which he used as a spittoon for the tobacco chaw bulging in his cheek.

"With all due respect, lieutenant, but are you suggesting the crew was beamed off the ship by a flying saucer or something?"

Strange stiffened.

"Now, senior chief, you have some respect for our new L-T," said Stalk.

It is naval tradition for chief petty officers to break in young officers, to guide them in their development as leaders. But in Lieutenant Strange's case, Chief Stalk took it to an extreme. Despite her all-business attitude, the childless electronics expert took what could not be described as anything but a motherly concern toward the young officer, providing a source of embarrassment for Strange and of good-natured mirth for the rest of the team.

"Ignore the nasty senior chief, lieutenant. Go on with what you were saying."

"I didn't mean that way," Strange said. "But now that you mention it, senior chief, can you explain how the DSV crew left the submarine *while it was submerged*?"

Hopper opened his mouth, then closed it, and shook his head.

"No, sir," he said.

"If it were easily explained," said Gates, "we wouldn't be here."

"In some ways, this whole thing reminds me of the Baychimo," said Brown.

At six-foot-three, the gunner's mate and explosives expert was the team's tallest member. Despite his lanky appearance, he was also the most muscular. Like Hopper, his thinning hair was cut close to the scalp. His light skin was creased and sun reddened. Brown, cautious eyes hid beneath a dark brow.

The lieutenant raised his eyebrows. "Baychimo?"

Brown looked at Gates.

"You brought it up, petty officer," Gates said. "You tell the story."

"Yes, sir," Brown said. He cleared his throat. "The merchant ship Baychimo was a cargo steamer built in the early 1900s. In 1931, she was plying her trade between American and Canadian waters when she became stuck in the ice not far from Barrow, Alaska. They expected the ice would crush the ship, abandoned her, and hiked to Barrow. They went back a couple days later to see if she was still afloat, and she was. They boarded her and got her underway, but she got stuck again. Half the crew gave up and left. The rest built a base camp near the ship to wait out the winter. A storm came up, and the Baychimo disappeared."

"Disappeared?" said Strange. "You mean she vanished?"

Brown held up his hand.

"Well, the crew believed she finally sank," he said. "But a few days later, native Inuits reported seeing the Baychimo nearly 50 miles away. The remaining crew found her and rowed out to board her, but a fog bank rolled in . . . and she disappeared again. Ever since, every few years the Baychimo reappeared. Not an image, sir. Not a spectral manifestation. But the real ship. There are actual photos of her, sir. The last reported sighting was in 1969, thirty-eight years after her first disappearance. For all we know, she's still afloat somewhere out here."

Strange looked at the senior chief, then at Gates.

"Is he pulling my leg, commander?"

"Nope," Gates said, shaking his head. "True story. It's not all that unknown in these waters. In 1775, the schooner Octavius was found in ice near Greenland. She was in good shape, but her crew was dead and their bodies frozen. Her log said the captain entered the Arctic from the Pacific seeking the Northwest Passage. The last log entry positioned them a couple hundred miles from Barrow and was dated 1761. With a dead crew, the Octavius somehow found her way through the frozen Arctic, something that wouldn't happen again until the USS Nautilus crossed the Arctic submerged."

Strange pondered the story, then nodded.

"I was thinking this was similar to the Mary Celeste," he said, referring to the legendary merchant sailing ship discovered abandoned in the Atlantic Ocean in 1872, the ship's boat gone, and food still on the dining table.

"Did you notice as we flew in that the Franklin's lifeboat is missing from the davits?" Gates asked.

17

Strange nodded. "Like the Mary Celeste," he said.

"Well, the Mary Celeste was probably abandoned because she carried a volatile cargo of grain alcohol that leaked and filled the cargo spaces with explosive fumes," Gates said. "At least that's what the board of inquiry determined. What we need to do is determine what made the Franklin's crew abandon her."

"But the Franklin isn't carrying any cargo," the lieutenant said.

"Exactly," Gates said. "So, I want a stem-to-stern search of this ship—every compartment, the bilges, even shaft alley. I used the sat phone to give the admiral a SITREP. He said the Navy is sending out a CIVMAR crew—civilian mariners—to salvage this ship. They should arrive first thing tomorrow. Before they arrive, I want to know if there is something aboard this ship so dangerous that maybe *we* shouldn't stay on board."

Gates stood and the rest followed. The commander held up two fingers and twisted them in the air.

"So, turn to," he said.

Chapter 4

T he summer sun never sets above the Arctic Circle. Even at midnight, it sits just above the horizon, casting the frigid sea, land, and ice fields into a semi-gloom usually seen during an early morning sunrise rather than the middle of the night. Gates paced the bridge deck of the Franklin, blaming the midnight sun on his sleepless night. But the midnight sun was not the reason for his being awake at this hour.

He had the dream again.

No, not a dream. A nightmarish memory of another night years before when, sleepless, he paced another deck at this hour. That night, however, was the complete opposite of this one—pitch black with no moon, and clouds covering the stars. And hot.

He was a lieutenant then, senior grade, one step up from young Leland Strange. It was shortly after the U.S. invasion of Iraq in 2003. Gates was in charge of a Coast Guard port security detachment protecting an Iraqi gas and oil platform. Called a GOPLAT, it served as a collection and distribution center for Iraqi ocean oil drilling operations. Earlier in the war, Navy SEALs and Coalition special forces captured the platforms before Saddam Hussein could order them destroyed. Afterward, Coast Guard port security units, or PSUs, took responsibility for protecting them from insurgent attacks.

It was god-awful duty. The GOPLATs were filthy and overrun with rats, forcing the Coasties to jury-rig hammocks between pipes to avoid waking up covered by the vermin. The stench of raw crude permeated everything, including the MRE ration packets. There were too few PSUs for the maritime security needs of the war, so they were broken up into detachments, undermanned and under-gunned. Each detachment had two 25-foot Boston Whaler gunboats, vessels too small to function effectively—or safely—in the open ocean. Called Guardians, the small boats carried one M2 .50 caliber machine gun forward and two M240 SAWs mounted port and starboard, and nothing else. On the platform itself were two sand-bagged heavy weapons emplacements, one for an M2 and the other for a Mark 19 grenade launcher. Gates wished he had a couple of heavy riverine command boats used by the Navy and armed with more modern grenade launchers and multiple machine guns, including a mini-gun with a devastating rate of fire. Hell, the Coast Guard ran the Riverine Warfare school at Camp Lejeune in North Carolina. Gates always wondered why the Coast Guard could never get those boats?

Nor was GOPLAT safe duty. Insurgents targeted the platforms with suicide boats, high-speed dhows laden with explosives. One Coastie had already been killed along with a Navy sailor during an insurgent attack on a similar platform. Gates had no intention of letting that happen to any of his men.

That night in the Persian Gulf, Gates had been staring into the dark when a flicker of light caught his attention. It was there, then gone. Then it was there again. He watched it for several minutes as it grew in intensity, then fade again. He climbed a ladder to one of the heavy-weapons emplacements and borrowed a set of night-vision goggles from the man on watch. Retracing his steps, he focused the NVGs on the mysterious light. It was brighter, even without the light-enhancing NVGs, but it still grew and faded. Gates assumed it was a vessel, but it appeared to zigzag as if avoiding submarines. Or maybe it was tacking with the wind. A sailing ship?

As the vessel drew closer, Gates realized it was a sailing vessel, but unlike any he had ever seen. Instead of running lights, the light he had first noticed was from the glow of the ship itself. To the naked eye, it was a soft bluish-white luminescence that engulfed the entire vessel. The ship was ancient, reminiscent of those tourist pirate ships plying the inshore waters of harbors back in the States. Ragged, torn sails billowed from three square-rigged masts, even though there was no wind that night.

The name of the ship struck him like a blow. *The Flying Dutchman*.

There had been a Gates or a Munro in the Coast Guard since the 19th century when it was still two separate entities, the U.S. Lifesaving Service and the Revenue Cutter Service. He grew up on sea lore and its mysteries. It was the love of those stories that drove Gates to earn a graduate degree in maritime archeology. He knew the myth of the Flying Dutchman, the ancient sea captain who cursed God and was condemned to sail the seas for eternity, never making landfall. According to the legend, sighting the Dutchman was a harbinger of disaster.

As a scientist, Gates understood the Flying Dutchman was simply a fable. As a mariner and descendant of mariners, he knew many right-minded men of the sea who claimed they saw the specter themselves. Lighthouse keepers at the Cape Point Lighthouse in South Africa claimed to have seen the Dutchman many times, always during deadly storms. German Admiral Karl Doenitz once said many of his U-boat crews reported seeing the Dutchman while on patrols during WWII, often before torpedoing a ship. Even British King George V saw the Dutchman, along with a dozen shipmates, when he was a Royal Navy midshipman on the HMS Bacchante. The sighting was duly recorded in the ship's log. Within hours a sailor on the Bacchante fell from a mast to his death. Sightings and disaster.

Gates clambered up the ladders to the where the GO-PLAT's control center stood. He sounded the platform's fire alarm, to which he had trained his men to respond to as a battle klaxon. He picked the microphone to the public-address system.

"General quarters. General quarters," he said, his voice booming across the platform. "All hands man your battle stations. Boat crews man your boats. This is not a drill."

Confused voices and the hollow ring of heavy boots on steel deck plates and stairs shattered the stillness of the night. The double slap of the Ma-Deuce machine gun bolts being rammed home echoed across the platform, joined by the lighter sound of the SAW bolts being worked. From below came the whine and roar of the twin 200-horse power outboard motors coming to life on the Guardians.

"What is it, sir?" asked the detachment's chief, as he snapped the chinstrap to his Kevlar helmet.

Gates was putting on his own kit.

"Don't know, chief," he said. "But there's something out there."

Gates picked up a hand-held radio and thumbed the push-to-talk button.

"Boat crews, stand out one hundred yards," he said.

The growl of the outboards responded as the boats veered away from the GOPLAT at high speed, their phosphorescent wakes gleaming against the dark plain of the sea.

A radio operator stepped from the platform's control room.

"L-T, Old Kentucky reports three inbounds from the east. High speed. Three hundred yards."

Old Kentucky was the call sign for a Navy mobile inshore undersea warfare unit on shore. Equipped with a variety of sensors, including radar and sonar, it acted as the eyes for the Coast Guard detachments guarding Iraqi offshore oil platforms.

"Jesus, they just pick them up now?"

"Yes, sir," the radioman said. "Kentucky said those dhows can get lost in sea clutter until they go to high speed. They're inbound now, sir."

Gates raised the hand-held and directed his small boats onto an intercept course.

The men on the platform could see the gunfire before they could hear it. Muzzle flashes and tracer rounds stabbed through the night, followed seconds later with the slow, steady hammering of the .50 calibers and the sharper staccato of the lighter SAWs. They also heard the distinctive clatter of the Kalashnikovs, the Russian-designed AK-47 assault rifles used by insurgents and terrorists around the world. There was another, heavier firing that Gates knew meant at least one of the enemy boats had something larger than an AK.

After only a minute they could see the boats, the muzzle flashes offering a choppy view of the firefight like an early black-and-white motion picture. One of the insurgent boats abruptly went dead in the water, its engine disabled by gunfire or its helmsman killed. Automatic fire still flashed from the boat until silenced by a Guardian's Ma-Deuce.

The remaining two insurgents continued their run for the platform, chased by the two Coast Guard boats. One Guardian gained on the enemy boats, its bow-mounted .50 caliber hammering at the nearest insurgent. Gates saw the Guardian was getting too close to the enemy vessel, a boat no doubt filled with explosives. Before he could radio a warning, a blast shattered the dark and lit up the surrounding water.

"No!"

Gates' heart sank at the thought of his own men caught up in that explosion. Then the pursuing Guardian plowed through the geyser of water and both Coast Guard boats charged after the last insurgent.

"Thank god," Gates muttered.

Two down but there was still the last insurgent boat, and it was getting close enough to threaten the platform. Gates ordered every man on the platform to open fire on it. A thunderous cacophony of heavy and light gun fire erupted from the GOPLAT. Fifty-caliber bullets raked the dhow. NATO 5.56mm rounds from the SAWs and M16 rifles showered it, but still the insurgent sped toward the platform. Grenades from the Mark 19 straddled the boat, raising geysers of spray, until one slammed into it amidships.

A volcanic geyser of water rose from the ocean's surface, carrying splinters of wood and metal, and pieces of human grist. It fell across the platform, the metal decks, and ladders; pipes pinged from the debris. Then the geyser subsided, and the night fell quiet except for the growl of the returning Guardians, and the sound of ringing in everyone's ears.

Chapter 5

C ommander?"
The voice of Leland Strange stirred Gates from his memories and drew him back from the Persian Gulf to the Arctic Ocean.

"Oh, Leland," Gates said. "I didn't hear you coming."

"Can't sleep, sir?" Strange asked.

Gates nodded, not feeling like explaining his dream to the young man. "Must be this midnight sun. All this light screws up my sleep cycle."

"It's pitch black below decks, sir. No electricity."

Gates had no reply. His lips opened and closed like a fish's mouth.

"It's okay, sir," Strange said. "With me being the new kid on the block and this my first mission, I figured you'd be checking up on me and make sure I didn't screw up on my first watch by falling asleep or something."

Gates felt relief. The young lieutenant had given him a way to change the topic.

"Yes, well, speaking of which," Gates said. "You handled yourself well today. I want you to know the only reason I wanted you with me when we searched ship was simply because it *is* your first mission. To break you in. It wasn't because I think you're inexperienced or—"

"Too young, sir?"

Gates looked at Strange. Even in the dusk of the midnight sun, he looked too young—younger than Gates could ever remember being.

"How old are you again?" Gates asked.

"Twenty-one, sir."

Gates did the math in his head. To receive a commission in the Coast Guard—or any other branch of the service—you needed at least a bachelor's degree. For most people, that meant not being eligible until they were at least twenty-one or twenty-two. And Leland Strange had far more than a bachelor's degree.

"And you already have a doctorate in oceanography?"

Strange nodded.

"And a master's in marine biology and another master's in chemistry?"

"How old were you when you graduated from high school?"

"Thirteen and a half, sir," Strange said, embarrassed by the question. "Almost fourteen, sir."

"Why aren't you teaching college somewhere?" Gates asked.

Strange leaned his arms on the ship's railing. The question was not new to him.

"Well, sir, I was offered two professorships," he said. "But I realized I'd spend the rest of my life in a classroom and . . . well, I've already spent my life up to now in classrooms. As a professor, I'd spend much of my time trying to raise grant money so I could spend two or three weeks at sea each year doing research—and then only if I was lucky enough to raise the money. The Coast Guard seemed a better way to get underway and perform research. The Guard does a lot of oceanic research and protection."

"Admiral Rickert recruited you, didn't he?"

"Yes, sir," Strange said. "I met him when I was doing my doctoral thesis. He was on my review board. How did you know?"

"It sounded like the same talk he gave me when he recruited me for this team."

Both men chuckled. Admiral Rickert was long retired from the Coast Guard, but no one dared not call him by his former rank. Rickert worked for the service as a civilian employee, and Deployable Specialized Force–Papa was his special project.

As a young officer, Rickert commanded a Coast Guard 82-foot patrol boat in Vietnam. On the night of June 15, 1968, two unknown aircraft attacked and sank a Navy swift boat while it was on coastal patrol. Rickert's boat was nearby and picked up the only two survivors. As the Coast Guard vessel hove to, another Navy Swift boat arrived.

Then the mysterious aircraft returned.

They appeared as lights hovering at low altitude a few hundred yards away. No one waited for another attack. Both boats opened fire on the objects. The heavy machine gun and cannon fire had little impact on the intruders, which turned and moved out to sea at high speed. Later that night, unidentified aircraft attacked an Australian Navy ship, killing one crewman and wounding several more. The Australian sailors never saw their attackers, neither by sight nor by radar.

Investigations into the events failed to identify the attackers. Friendly fire attacks by Navy and Air Force aircraft on allied patrol boats and ships were not unknown. But there were no friendly aircraft in the area at the time. Investigators concluded the attackers were "enemy helicopters," a conclusion that was no conclusion at all.

The fact was the small North Vietnamese air force had few helicopters, and those it had were lumbering transports, not high-speed gunships. Even if it had attack choppers, no combat aircraft flies at night in a war zone with their navigation lights illuminated. The victims of the attacks also knew "enemy helicopters" was the military code word for unidentified flying objects—UFOs—precisely because the North Vietnamese choppers never engaged in combat. The experience left Admiral Rickert with a life-long belief that mysterious things occurred at sea, things that required investigation if for no other reason than to maintain the safety of mariners.

"Is it true what I heard about why the admiral chose you, sir?" Strange asked.

Though unseen in the dim light, the smile fled Gates' face.

"What have you heard?" he asked, teeth clenched.

"That you have a psychic gift," the lieutenant said. "That at the Battle of the GOPLAT, you had a forewarning of the attack that allowed you to prepare for it."

"And who told you that?"

"Members of the team," Strange said. "They say you saw the Flying Dutchman and recognized it as a sign of foreboding."

In the aftermath of the battle, Gates never mentioned the mysterious ship in his after-action report. There was an alert from the Navy MIUW unit, he wrote. He deployed his boats and manned defenses on the platform and destroyed the enemy. Injuries to personnel were slight and damage to the platform inconsequential. But Gates' commander knew Gates deployed his people *before* the Navy unit issued its warning and demanded to know how he anticipated the attack. Trying to avoid the truth, Gates said he simply had a hunch. That's all, a hunch.

Yet, that was enough to earn him a reputation as a soothsayer, the junior officer who could tell the future. During a night of drinking after his deployment, Gates let slip his sighting of the Flying Dutchman. The Coast Guard is a small service. Five deployed Navy aircraft carriers have more people on board them than the entire Coast Guard has uniformed personnel. It wasn't long before word spread about Gates' experience with the paranormal. Gates assumed his career was finished. Instead, it brought him to Admiral Rickert's attention.

He sighed.

"Lieutenant," he said, "I have no idea what I saw that night—if anything at all. I was tired and under a lot of stress. We all were. It's possible, in my exhaustion, I had a hallucination or maybe saw a mirage. In that part of the world, people see Fata Morganas all the time."

A Fata Morgana was an optical illusion, seen along the ocean's horizon, created by the refraction of light through layers of air with differing temperatures. A Fata Morgana can make an unseen ship far below the horizon appear as a ghostly specter floating above it.

"Whatever it was," Gates continued, "hallucination or mirage, it created in me a deep foreboding. And that was what I acted on—the foreboding, not the sighting."

"Yes, sir," Strange said. He fell silent for a while, then said, "But it could have been."

"Could have been what?" Gates snapped. His hands gripped the railing. Rickert had said the same thing.

"The Flying Dutchman," the young officer said. "Mysterious things happen at sea, don't they, sir? I mean, that's why we're standing here on the deck of a ship that disappeared five days ago and reappeared without its crew. Add to that a submersible that disappeared and reappeared without its crew."

"You're making my head hurt, Leland."

"Sorry, sir."

Gates let the topic drop and brought up another. He nodded toward a bright light in the distance.

"That must be that Russian oil-drilling platform," he said. "What's it called again?"

"The Vilanovsky, sir," Strange said. He had no problem with the pronunciation. "It's one of Russia's new year-round, ice-resistant rigs they designed to take advantage of polar melting due to climate change."

"Came up here once on an ice breaker years ago," Gates said, shaking his head. "It was beautiful, pristine. The ice shelves thick and awe-inspiring. A few more years of this and it'll look like the Gulf of Mexico."

"Worse, sir," Strange said. "There's less water circulation in the Arctic than in the gulf. If there's a spill here, it will stay here."

Chapter 6

T he first airlift of CIVMARS arrived as soon as there was enough light to land. CIVMARs, or civilian mariners, were government employees hired by the Navy's Military Sealift Command, or MSC, to operate its auxiliary ships. Chief among these were the tankers and cargo ships that sailed with strike groups and task forces, and kept the warships fed, fueled, and stocked with ammunition. However, they also included hospital ships, submarine tenders, rescue and salvage vessels, and test and research ships.

The CIVMARs came in a helicopter able to land on the small helo pad forward of the bridge. Four people stepped from the aircraft. Three wore khaki uniforms covered by foul-weather jackets; one wore a blue jumpsuit, also covered by a cold-weather coat. They took sea bags, rucksacks, and well-worn luggage from the helicopter, hefted them and, stooping, moved out from under the aircraft's rotating blades toward where Gates and Strange waited. The man in the lead was older than the rest, with a short white beard that stood out against his sun-bronzed face. His eyes were a shade of sea gray. He wore a blue ball cap on which Gates recognized the silver eagle showing the rank of captain in both the Coast Guard and Navy, though this eagle had a bar across it, engraved with the letters MSC. Gates wasn't certain he needed to salute the man—who was technically a civilian—but he did so as a courtesy.

"Welcome aboard, captain," Gates said. His salute returned, the two men shook hands. "I'm Lieutenant Commander Gates, U.S. Coast Guard. This is my second-in-command, Lieutenant Strange."

"T. L. Gunnar," the man said. His voice was strong and powerful, a voice used to the sea. The second man in khaki stepped up beside Gunnar. He had dark, clean-cut, Hispanic features and black hair flecked with gray. "My chief mate, Geraldo Salcedo."

Salcedo shook Gates' and Strange's hands. "Call me Gerry."

"We're a bit less formal with titles in the CIVMARs," Gunnar said.

"Doug," Gates said. He gestured to Strange. "Leland."

"But you can still call me 'Captain,'" Gunnar added, with a wry smile. He looked Strange over and said, "They cut them young these days, don't they?"

"I think you'll find Lieutenant Strange is a young man with multiple talents. I don't even know them all yet." Gates paused as the last two civilian mariners approached. "This isn't your entire crew, is it, captain?"

"No, no," said Gunnar, "just my advanced team to pave the way for the rest of my crew. They'll be coming in relays over the next few hours. Twenty-four of us, all together."

The third man in khakis stepped up, and Gates saw by the cut of his side pockets he wore a coverall rather than shirt and pants. He had a light-brown, unruly beard and faded blue eyes. A navy-blue wool watch cap pulled low over his ears displayed a ship's propeller surrounded by a wreath.

"My chief engineer, Jack Weil," Gunnar said. "And this . . ." The captain gestured to the fourth and final CIVMAR. ". . . is my DSV operator, Sarah Sandford."

Gates did his best to hide his reaction to the tall, beautiful, black woman. Her skin was a rich mahogany, and her eyes deep, dark, and fathomless. Despite the blue coveralls and foul-weather jacket she wore, it was obvious she was slender and athletic, and, from her handshake, strong. She removed a dark-blue watch cap and ran fingers through short, black curls flecked with red. Her smile was wide, sensuous, and inviting. It nearly took Gates' breath away.

"I brought Sarah in early to look at that DSV," Gunnar said, "and try to get a grasp on what happened to its crew. That is how this started, isn't it?"

"Yes, it is, captain," Gates stammered. "Good idea. Welcome aboard, Miss Sanford."

"Just call me Sarah," Sandford said. "And you, lieutenant, can stop staring at me like that."

Gates glanced at the young officer. His mouth was slack and the eyes behind his horn-rimmed glasses bulged.

"Lieutenant Strange," Gates said, snapping the young man out of his catatonia, "why don't you help Miss Sandf— Sarah with her gear?"

Sandford had a duffel, a rucksack, and what appeared to be a laptop case draped over her shoulders. Leland Strange rushed the woman, eager to relieve her of her burden.

"*At ease*, lieutenant," Sandford said, stepping back. "I can carry my own gear." She side-stepped Strange, who stood frozen with his arms outstretched, and smiled at Gates. "But I appreciate the offer, commander. I don't get such consideration from the men I usually work with." She smiled again, glancing at Gunnar and the other CIVMARs. Then she slipped past Gates and headed inside the ship.

"Don't believe her," Gunnar said, chuckling. "Sarah doesn't need help for anything. Born to the sea, that one.

Now, if you don't mind, Doug, let's get our gear stowed in quarters and then you can brief us on what we have here."

Fifteen minutes later the CIVMARs, Gates, and Strange were sitting in the ship's conference room. Gates had given up to Gunnar the captain's quarters he slept in the night before and took one of the scientists' cabins. Gunnar—used to being the one in charge—had taken the chair at the head of the conference table.

"As far as we can tell, the ship is totally dead," Gates said. "The generators aren't working and, of course, neither are the engines. She's adrift and not under command."

As if to stress the point, the Franklin—pushed by a beam sea—took a steep roll to starboard. Gunnar turned toward his chief mate.

"Gerry, as soon as the deck department gets aboard, rig out an anchor. The sea depth isn't that deep. A couple of shackles worth—30 fathoms—should do it. That should stabilize the ship until we can get some way on."

"Aye, sir," Salcedo said.

Gunnar turned to Weil, his chief engineer.

"Jack, get the generators on line," he said. "We can't fix anything until we get more light. We're blind and deaf, too, without radar or communications."

"I have comms, captain." Gates pulled out the sat phone.

"Yes, I have one, too," Gunnar said. "But at these latitudes even sat phones are problematic."

Gates nodded, then said to Weil, "Senior Chief Hopper is my engineer. I'm certain he'd be happy to assist you."

"Thank you, Doug," Weil said.

"In the event we can't get the Franklin underway again, I've arranged for a sea-going tug to tow us in," Gunnar said. "Unfortunately, the only tugs big enough and near enough are busy towing a damaged oil platform into Point Barrow. I'm afraid if we can't get underway ourselves, we could be here for several days."

"Understood, captain," Gates said. "Of course, my team will stay aboard. We need to complete our investigation and, in light of what happened aboard this ship, I think you could use the security."

"Thank you, Doug," Gunnar said. "Sarah, you know what I need you to do. Check over that DSV and see if you can find something that might clear up this mystery."

Sandford nodded. "Yes, captain."

"Captain, I'd like Lieutenant Strange to accompany Sarah," Gates said. "Anything she might find would have a direct bearing on our mission here."

Gunnar nodded. "Make it so, Sarah."

Sandford regarded Strange the way a parent would an upstart child.

"I don't suppose you've ever been on a submersible, lieutenant?" she asked.

"Yes, I have . . . Sarah," he said. "I made a couple of dives on Alvin when I was studying at Woods Hole. And please call me Leland."

Sandford stared at Strange, her mouth agape.

"Lieutenant Strange . . . Leland . . . has a PhD in oceanography," Gates said, struggling to contain his grin. "Along with a few other degrees and honors. If you have trouble calling him Leland, I'm sure doctor will suffice."

The three remaining CIVMARs mimicked Sandford's face. Sandford nodded and shrugged. "All right then, let's go see the DSV."

As they left, Salcedo and Weil also requested leave to depart. Gates stood, ready to leave, but Gunnar asked him to stay.

The merchant captain settled back into his chair and regarded Gates with his sea-gray eyes.

"Lieutenant Commander Douglas Munro Gates," he said, emphasizing Gate's first and middle names.

"Sir?"

"You know, Doug, when you graduate from the U.S. Merchant Marine Academy, as I did, you're required to hold a reserve commission in one of the armed forces for six years. I chose the Coast Guard, because it seemed best suited for the work I planned to do as a career. Got called up for Operation Desert Storm in '91. So, I'm well aware of who Douglas Munro was. A relative?"

Signalman 1st Class Douglas Munro was a legend in the Coast Guard as the only member of the service ever awarded the Medal of Honor. After the Battle of Savo Island in 1942, the Navy retreated from Guadalcanal, leaving the Marines stranded. A large number of Coast Guardsmen, however, chose to remain with the Leathernecks. Those who crewed landing craft used their boats to shuttle troops and supplies around the island. Those without boats picked up rifles and joined infantry units.

On September 27, a small flotilla of landing craft commanded by Munro landed three companies of Marines on the beach at Point Cruz. The Marines quickly found themselves outnumbered by Japanese troops and pushed back toward the sea. Munro led his small flotilla back to Point Cruz to evacuate the Americans. As the Marines were being loaded onto the boats, Munro positioned his own vessel between them and withering Japanese machine gun fire. Miraculously, every Marine was rescued. But as the boats made their escape, one became disabled and came under heavy fire. Munro again positioned his boat in the line of fire. Both Munro's boat and the disabled vessel escaped but Munro paid the ultimate price. The Navy had long refused to award the Medal of Honor to any Coast Guardsman going back to the Spanish-American War, but in Munro's case the Marines insisted the Navy award him the honor.

"A distant cousin, sir," Gates said. "But how did you know my middle name, captain? I don't recall introducing myself that way when you came on board."

Captain Gunnar gave Gates that wry smile.

"You know Admiral Rickert, don't you?" Gates guessed.

"I served with him during Desert Storm," he said, nodding. "He was just a captain back then. He called me the other day when he learned I was being assigned to salvage the Franklin. Told me about your little group. What's it called again? Deployable Operational Group–Papa?"

"That was the old name, captain," Gates said, grimacing. "It had the unfortunate acronym of DOG–P."

The old seaman guffawed and slapped the table. "DOG–P! That certainly is an unfortunate acronym!"

The captain's laughter was contagious and Gates found himself joining in it.

"Well, that's an interesting line of work you're in," Gunnar said after the laughter subsided. "Chasing down mysteries at sea and all."

"To be honest," Gates said, "the mysteries aren't always that mysterious. Most have a simple explanation. But we look into anything that might have an impact on maritime trade."

"And as a merchant seaman, I thank you for that," Gunnar said. "But I suspect there are plenty of mysteries you can't find an easy answer to."

He leaned forward in his chair, placing his arms on the table.

"I've been going to sea for more than thirty years, Doug. And we merchant sailors spend a great deal more time underway than you military sailors. There's no profit in having a cargo ship tied up to the dock for any length of time. I can tell you, in all those years, I've seen some strange things. I'm not talking about St. Elmo's Fire. I'm talking about strange lights in the night sky—and under the water. A roiling sea surrounded by dead flat water. Fogs that rise from nowhere and disappear again. Hell, strange vessels that suddenly appear on a collision course looking as solid as this tub, yet we see nothing on radar, and then they just disappear. When they briefed me on this job, and they told me what had happened to the Franklin, I can tell you I really wasn't the least bit shocked. Mysterious things happen at sea, Doug. Mysterious things."

Gunnar fell silent. His eyes focused elsewhere. He shook his head.

"Ah, but I prattle on," he said. "I'm sure you think I'm just an old salt-encrusted fool ready for the scrapyard."

"Not at all, sir," Gates protested. "I feel much the same as you. I've . . . experienced things, too."

"Well, one of these days when we're back on shore, perhaps we'll raise a pint or two and see who can tell the biggest lie," Gunnar said, smiling. He stood. "In the meanwhile, I have a ship to salvage and you have a mystery to solve."

Chapter 7

Gates stepped out of the bridge and turned the collar of his foul-weather jacket up against the chilled Arctic air. He took the ladder to the main deck and headed toward the Franklin's stern.

The DSV sat beneath the A-frame. It was larger than Gates expected and reminded him of a cross between a submarine and an insect. Topside, the submersible had the vague shape of a sub, with a yellow rounded hull topped by a flat deck striped with black non-skid. A small orange conning tower rose from the deck forward of the vessel's midline.

That was where any comparison to the submarines Gates knew ended.

Below the yellow hull was a Plexiglas bubble and two spidery mechanical arms tipped with pincer-like claws. Mounted on each side of the DSV were two small thrusters—propellers encased in cone-shaped housings. Mounted beneath the hull were two skids similar to those on certain light helicopters. Stenciled on the bow in large block letters was "CHIP-1."

Gates found Strange and Sandford looking underneath the DSV.

"Anything?" Gates asked.

Strange straightened at the sound of Gates' voice.

"No, sir," he said. "But Sarah and I just started looking. We decided to look through the sub's—"

"DSV," Sandford corrected.

"Look through the DSV's hangar first," Strange continued, "but we didn't find anything unusual."

"Well, then, carry on," Gates said.

Gates heard a grunt from above. Sandford had climbed onto the DSV and was trying to undog the entry hatch. She looked at the men. "One of you big hunky men want to grab a dogging wrench and help me get this damn thing open?" she asked. "It's stuck."

Strange dashed into the hangar, eager to retrieve the wrench. When he returned, Gates was standing on the submersible's deck, a hand extended to receive the tool.

"Thank you, lieutenant," Gates said, before turning back to Sandford.

"Yes, sir," Strange said, his words sagging with disappointment.

Gates stuck the wrench into the dogging wheel and, with Sandford pulling and him pushing, the wheel turned.

"It's not supposed to be that hard to turn," Sandford said, pulling the hatch open. She studied the hatch's latches, and its knife edge and the rubber it bit into and grunted. "It looks off kilter, as if someone tried to force it."

She dropped one leg into the hatch, then the other, and disappeared into the sub. A moment later, her head reappeared. "Coming, commander?"

Gates lowered himself into the mini-sub. Light filtered into the interior from two small lateral-view ports and the Plexiglas window. Sandford sat in a reclining pilot seat, one of two squeezed into the cramped pressure hull. A third person could lie on a padded bench between the seats. Gates slid into the second chair.

"Ever been in one of these before?" Sandford asked as she started throwing switches.

"No," he said. "I'm a qualified diver. Have to be to be a marine archeologist. But I've never been in a submersible before."

He turned and found Sandford starting at him.

"What?"

"A marine archeologist?" Sandford said. "And an oceanographer? What kind of Coast Guard team are you?"

"A well-educated one," Gates said. "The bow stencil—Chip-1. Is that its name?"

"Yup," Sandford said, her hands playing over the controls, flipping switches. "There are three DSVs in this class, Chip-1, Chip-2, and Chip-3, named after the father of all DSVs, Alvin—you know, the one Robert Ballard used to find the Titanic."

She glanced at Gates. He shrugged.

"Commander," she said, "you mean you've never heard of Alvin and the Chipmunks?"

Footsteps thudded above them, and Leland Strange's face appeared in the hatch.

"Skipper, Chief Hopper is trying to contact you," he said. "The radio signal must not be penetrating the DSV's hull."

"What's he got?" Gates asked.

"He said he needs you in main engineering right away. He and the CIVMAR engineer found something in the shaft alley."

"Tell him I'm on my way." Gates glanced at Sanford. "Sorry."

"Don't mind me," she said, flashing that smile that entranced him. "I've got my baby sub to keep me occupied."

"DSV," Gates corrected, smiling. He stood, climbed through the hatch, and jumped to the deck. Strange hovered over the hatch, expecting—or hoping—for an invitation from Sanford.

"Leland, stay outside the DSV in case I need to call you on the radio," Gates said as he trotted forward toward the deck house.

Strange sighed, sat on the mini-sub's deck, and sullenly sank his chin into his palms.

On older ships, the propeller shaft runs from the ship's engine through a tunnel to the point where it penetrates the hull via a waterproof packing case and attaches to the propeller, also known as the screw. This is shaft alley.

The Franklin, however, was of a modern design, only out of the yard for a couple of years. Instead of screws and rudders, twin azimuth thrusters propelled and steered the ship. Rotating pods beneath the ship's stern housed the propellers and their electric motors. Mechanical servos inside the engine room turned each pod three hundred and sixty degrees, allowing the steering of the ship without the need for a rudder. Electricity generated by a diesel-electric system powered the pods' motors and the servos. Hence, the Franklin had no shaft alley, but in the maritime service old terms die hard.

The lights were still out below decks. Jack Weil met Gates at the stairs leading to the engine room. Weil wore a headlamp and used it to guide Gates into the depths of the Franklin's mechanical heart. The only light in the spaces came from emergency lanterns. Despite the dim lighting, Gates saw a modern engine compartment more akin to the control room of a nuclear power station than the hot, grease-encrusted caverns he saw as a youth visiting the Coast

Guard cutters his father served aboard. Computer screens, blank and lifeless, lined the control center. Gauges and readout screens, just as dead, glinted under the swaying beams of light.

"No luck on getting the generator going?" Gates' breath turned to fog as he spoke. The ship's engineering space sat below the Franklin's waterline. Without power, it was colder in the engine room than topside.

"Haven't even tried yet," said Weil. "Can't do much until we fix this."

Weil shined his lamp light on an opened power panel. A rat's nest of wires dangled from the open doors.

"Someone tore this apart to kill power to the rest of the ship," he said. "Chief Hopper and I were looking for spare fuses and wiring when he found that."

Weil angled his head toward the rear of the compartment. Gates swung his flashlight around. Chief Hopper leaned against one of two blue safety railings encircling the large rectangular servos that rotated the propulsion pods. Hopper motioned Gates over.

Jess Brown squatted within the railing of the port-side servo, studying the base of the mechanism under the light of his own headlamp. Gates made a mental note to pull his own headlamp out of his kit.

"I don't know what made me come over here and look, but when I did, I found this," Hopper said. "I called Jess right after notifying Lieutenant Strange."

Brown stood and moved away from the servo, keeping his headlamp shining at the servo base where it connected to the propulsion pod through a watertight packing case. The lamp beam revealed a mound of gray, claylike material. A thin metal tube the width and length of a pencil protruded from the mound.

"Is that what I think it is?" Gates' voice was tight.

"Yes, sir," Brown said. "Plastic explosive. Shaped charge from the looks of it. With a timed pencil detonator."

"Jesus," Gates muttered. "If that goes off, it'll blow a hole right through the packing case and the hull."

"It gets worse," Hopper said.

He stepped over to the starboard set of turning gears and focused his headlamp on its base. Another explosive mound sat against its packing case, a pencil detonator jammed into its mass.

"That could be why the crew abandoned ship, sir." Hopper said. "Similar to the Mary Celeste."

Gates shook his head. "Maybe. But if they did, it means the crew is still floating around in the lifeboat. We'll have to notify the rescue coordination center to get the big birds flying again." Gates thought a moment, then asked, "Were the watertight doors set when you first came down here yesterday?"

"No, sir," Chief Hopper said. "They were wide open when we did our hasty search after coming aboard."

"If they were in fear of sinking, you'd think they'd set watertight integrity. The crew members were licensed mariners."

"Yes, sir."

"Excuse me. I'm no explosive expert," said Weil. "But could those things still go off?"

"Jess?" Gates asked.

"Pencil detonators don't have delays longer than twenty-four hours," Brown said. "Cold temperatures can sometimes lengthen that, but they should have blown long ago."

"So, they haven't been activated?" Gates asked.

"Oh, they've been activated," Brown said.

He focused the headlamp beam on one of the detonators. Its tip was crushed.

"Oldies but goodies," he said. "These things were first developed by the Brits in World War Two. They were so reliable and so easy to use, both sides used them. A glass vial in the top of the tube holds a corrosive liquid. When you crimp the end, it breaks that vial, releasing the corrosive. In time, it eats through a retaining wire holding back a spring-loaded firing pin. The firing pen slams forward into a percussion cap which sets off the blasting cap which detonates the explosive charge. The thickness of the wire determines the delay, from a few minutes to twenty-four hours. Roughly. They're still used today. The IEDs used in the Mumbai terrorist bombings in '08 had pencil detonators."

"So, these are duds," Weil said, his voice edged with hope.

Brown frowned.

"I don't believe they're duds," he said. "As I said, time pencils can be affected by weather. It's freezing in here. The corrosive liquid may have frozen in the vials. When the ends were crimped, the liquid didn't reach the retaining wires. At least that's my guess."

"Don't they use two detonators per bomb in case one doesn't work?" asked Gates.

"Yes, sir," the gunner's mate said. He shrugged. "Perhaps they figured if only one charge went off, sympathetic detonation would set off the second charge."

"Can we pull the detonators?" asked Gates.

"Well, sir, there we have a Devil's choice," Brown said. "If we pull them, the movement could cause the retaining wire to snap if there's been any corrosion. On the other hand, if we remove the whole charge—the plastic explosive with the detonators still in them—the same thing might happen."

"So, we just leave the bombs in place?"

"I wouldn't recommend that, sir," Brown said. "If and when we get power back on, this engine room will warm, and the corrosive will thaw . . ."

"And the bombs explode," concluded Gates. "Understood. We're damned if we do, damned if we don't."

"Yes, sir. As I said, sir, a Devil's choice."

"Your best advice, then?"

Brown bit his lip and scratched his head. Then he sighed.

"I'd say we remove the charge. There should be less movement to the detonators . . . if we're careful."

Gates thought it over, the muscles in his jaw flexing, then he nodded.

"Okay," he said. "Let's do it."

Chapter 8

G ates and Brown stood alone in main engineering. Gates sent Jack Weil and Senior Chief Hopper forward to muster with the rest of the CIVMARs and Coasties on the landing pad. Everyone forward wore their survival suits—mandatory equipment in Arctic waters. Without electricity to run the winches, the Franklin's two work boats—rigid-hull inflatables with outboard motors—were muscled into the water. Two life rafts stored on the O-1 deck in canisters with hydrostatic releases were broken out and laid on the deck. Every watertight door in the ship was closed and dogged.

Gates ordered the precautions in case their attempt to remove the bombs failed and they blew holes through the bottom of the Franklin. When Gates explained his plan to Leland Strange, the young officer protested.

"Sir, I should be the one to assist Jessie," he said. "As team leader, you're more valuable to this mission than I am."

Gates smiled at Strange.

"Leland, as an officer you need to learn that you never have someone else do something you wouldn't do yourself. Understand?"

The lieutenant nodded.

He sighed. "Understood, sir."

Neither Gates nor Brown bothered with a survival suit. If they failed, and one or both bombs exploded, the blast would kill them instantly or they'd drown when inundated with icy seawater.

Despite the chill, Gates wiped sweat from his upper lip. It dripped down his torso from beneath his arms. Gates noticed a similar effect on Brown's close-cropped hair as he climbed over the blue safety railing surrounding the port thruster servos and squatted before the first bomb.

Gates moved so he could focus his flashlight on the charge. Brown blew on his gloved hands, then looked at Gates.

"Here goes," he said, with a grim smile.

He reached out and touched the plastic explosive. His fingers flinched as if his touch might set the bomb off. He touched it again, his fingers gripping its edges, and pulled.

The charge lifted off the packing case, leaving behind only a small residue. He turned and showed it to Gates. Both men realized they were holding their breath and exhaled, their breath creating great billows of condensate. Brown stood with great caution and laid the bomb on top of the gear box.

"One down," he said.

Brown clambered over the guard rail, then over the railing of the starboard propulsion servo. Gates followed, using his flashlight to illuminate the bomb. This time, the plastique refused to come loose. Brown glanced at his team leader, but Gates urged him on. The gunner's mate adjusted this position and dug his gloved fingers into the plastique and gently rocked it. The movement caused the pencil detonator to tilt drunkenly. Brown froze.

"Careful," Gates said.

"Like I need to be reminded," Brown muttered.

Brown set back to work, rocking the charge until it loosened and came free. He lifted it and stood, facing Gates. Sweat streaked his face.

"Good work, Jess," Gates said. "Now let's get these things topside."

Brown stepped over the safety railing and waited as Gates retrieved the other bomb. They eased up the stairs leading out of the engineering, stopping at the top as Gates balanced his bomb in one arm and worked the dogging lever with the other. They went through, not bothering to close and dog it. A blast at that moment would do minimal damage to the ship. They repeated the motions with each hatch and scuttle they came to until they reached the main deck.

Once on deck, Gates quickstepped to the side of the ship and dropped his bomb over the side. Brown, eager to rid himself of his burden, trotted across the fantail. The quick movement jarred the loosened detonator. It fell from the explosive, clattering to the deck. Without thinking, Brown tossed his bomb overboard and both he and Gates threw themselves behind whatever cover they found. They turned and stared at the detonator as it rolled across the heaving deck.

Nothing happened.

The two men cursed, and—for the first time in what seemed hours—relaxed.

Then the detonator and blasting cap blew with a deafening crack, causing both men to jump. A splinter of shrapnel creased Brown's cheek, and he yelped. Gate's earpiece came alive with different voices calling him.

"Commander! Commander Gates!"

Gates thumbed the push-to-talk button. "We're okay. We're okay," he assured everyone on the net. "That was just a blasting cap. The bombs are overboard."

He glanced at Brown.

"Lieutenant Strange, send Chee to the fantail with his aid bag. Jess caught a piece of shrapnel in his cheek. And I want you to organize a thorough search of this ship, stem to stern. I want to know if there are any more bombs on board."

Gates dropped beside Brown, his back against the bulkhead. Brown was trying to staunch the flow of blood from his cheek with a gloved hand. Tension relieved, the sweat the both men produced in the engine room chilled their faces and necks. Looking at each other, they did what so many people do when they've come close to death.

They laughed.

Chapter 9

G ates hung up the sat phone, glanced at the drift ice surrounding the Franklin, then went into the ship's conference room. Captain Gunnar was sitting at the head of the table, typing on a laptop, the light from the computer screen illuminating his white beard. The only other light came from sunlight filtering through the portholes. Gates noticed a cable connecting the captain's laptop to his own sat phone, using it as a modem.

"I need to do that," he said. "I'm sick of filing SITREPS by text messages."

Gunnar chuckled.

"You have no idea how much paperwork this job involves, especially on a skeleton crew salvage like this," he said. "Speaking of which, my second flight of CIVMARs arrived. I've got Gerry getting them quartered, then they'll get to work on the anchor. Without propulsion, we'll have to let it drag until it catches, but it's the best we can do."

Gates nodded. "I saw the helo coming in when I was talking to the admiral."

"How is the admiral?"

"Not happy after hearing about those bombs," Gates said. "And the Navy is trying to horn in on our mission. Something about wanting to send their own team out to the Franklin. The admiral is pushing back hard on that."

"If I know Admiral Rickert, he'll win the pushing contest."

"I hope so," Gates said, his voice uncertain.

"Anyway, another helicopter is en route with the last of my crew," Gunnar said. "Then we can get some work done."

"Let me know if you need help from any of my people," Gates said.

"You've got enough headaches of your own to take care of, Doug," the merchant captain said. "Like making sure there's not another bomb on board. By the way, you handled that situation well. Bravo Zulu."

Bravo Zulu was the flag code abbreviation for "well done."

"Well, Jess Brown did the work," Gates said. "Guess I need to write him up for a commendation or something."

"I always thought a good bottle of whiskey was a better reward than a piece of colored ribbon."

"You may be right, captain."

"Any idea who planted the explosives?" Gunnar asked.

Gates rolled his stiff neck, then shook his head.

"I've been trying to figure that out," he said. "Down in the engine room, the senior chief speculated the explosives might be the reason the Franklin was abandoned. Perhaps like the crew of the Mary Celeste, the crew only meant to wait out the danger but got separated from the ship in a fog."

"That means a crew member placed the bombs," Gunnar said. "But why? An act of terrorism?"

"No," said Gates. "Terrorists prefer big audiences. Sinking a research ship at the remote top of the world wouldn't have the impact they seek from their acts. What about a disgruntled crewman?"

Gunnar set his elbows on the table and rested his chin on his clenched hands. "Maybe, but everyone on that crew was a licensed U.S. mariner. After 9/11, everyone gets a thorough background check. Each of my people have a security clearance."

"Your people work for the Navy," Gates said. "Most civilian jobs in the military required security clearances. But the Franklin was operated by an oceanographic institute. I can see its crew members having background checks, but security clearances?"

"The crew wasn't Navy, Doug, but the ship is owned by the Navy. It was only leased to the institute. That's why a Navy MSC salvage crew was sent bring her back."

Gunnar sat back in his chair and crossed his arms.

"Here's something else to consider, Doug," he said. "Those bombs were placed on the servos of the propulsion pods, right?"

Gates nodded.

"How could someone place those bombs without being seen by the engineering watch?"

Gates pictured the layout of main engineering. Unless he was part of the engineering staff, the saboteur had to pass the control room and the engineer on watch, cross to the servos, and place the bombs—all the time exposed in a well-lit machinery space. Not easy to do.

"I see your point," Gates said. "Maybe he disabled the engineering watch?"

"Then trashed the main engines and destroyed the electrical switch boxes, and calmly joined the rest of the crew—including the disabled watch staff since we haven't found them—and abandoned the ship in the lifeboat?"

Gates lips pursed as he nodded.

"Too much for one man?"

"Unless you believe President Kennedy was killed by a lone gunman," Gunnar said.

"That's what the history books say," Gates said, smiling.

The overhead florescent lights flickered once, twice, then caught, filling the dim compartment with light.

"Now we're making headway," said Gunnar, looking up at the brilliant overhead.

"Gates to Hopper," Gates said into his mini-boom mic. "Well done, senior chief."

"Don't thank me yet, skipper," Hopper said. "The latest group of CIVMARs brought the spare parts we needed to fix the electrical boards, and Mr. Weil and I got one emergency generator going, but not the main diesel electrics. We got electricity but not enough to power the thrusters."

"Keep at it, senior," Gates said, adding with a wink toward Gunnar, "And give Mr. Weil my compliments."

"Aye, sir," the senior chief said.

Gates turned back to Gunnar.

"I don't suppose you subscribe to the UFO theory?" he said.

"That the crew was kidnapped by aliens?" Gunnar gave Gates a bemused shake of his head. "I've told you before, Doug, mysterious things happen at sea. But in this case, I'm sure if someone boarded the Franklin, they were terrestrial, not extraterrestrial."

"But boarded by who? Pirates?"

Gunnar shrugged.

"Pirates infest every ocean on earth," he said. "Now that the polar melt is allowing more commercial traffic to ply these waters, why wouldn't piracy follow?"

Gates pondered the possibility. Gunnar was right. Modern day piracy was rampant throughout the world. Merchant ships often carried professional, well-armed security teams to protect the ships. Repel boarder drills were held as often as firefighting drills. There was no reason piracy wouldn't raise its ugly head in Arctic waters as commercial traffic increased.

"The problem with that, captain, is pirates usually hold the crew of captured ships for ransom. Or they kill the crew and sell the cargo, even the ship itself, on the black market. They don't sink the ships they capture."

Gunnar raised his hands in a gesture of frustration, a grin stretching beneath his snowy beard.

"Then I guess we're left with UFOs."

Gates chuckled. He stood and stepped to a porthole and stared out across the drift ice. "Maybe."

Lieutenant Strange entered the conference room, out of breath from running up ladders and stairs.

"I've got the team minus Senior Chief Hopper searching for more bombs, commander," he said, "but it's been slow going without light."

"How much have you cleared?"

"I had them concentrate on the third deck first," Strange said. "That deck is below the waterline and most vulnerable to a breach. They're nearly finished there and haven't found anything unusual. Now we have lights, it should go faster."

"Good thinking, Leland. Sit down."

The lieutenant pulled out a chair and sat.

"I just got off the sat phone with the admiral," Gates said. "I'm curious about that Russian drilling platform." He glanced at Gunnar, who raised his eyebrows and formed his mouth into an O as he understood Gates' reasoning. "As close as they are, they may have seen something around the Franklin before she disappeared. I thought I'd take one of the work boats and visit them. I asked the admiral to work with the State Department to get permission."

Strange nodded in agreement.

"I should go with you, sir."

"Negative. You should stay here in charge of the team," Gates said. "I'll take the senior chief. He might like to get a look at the engineering in that rig."

"Sir, I spent a summer studying oceanography in Moscow," the lieutenant said. "I spent several weeks on a Russian arctic oil rig studying its impact on the surrounding sea life. I know my way around a rig. Plus, I speak fluent Russian—one of several languages I speak."

Gates looked at the young officer, then at Gunnar. The old man's mouth curled with a wry smile.

"Of course, you do, lieutenant," Gates said. "I suspect that had something to do with the admiral recruiting you." Strange nodded. "Very well. It'll be a day or two before we receive permission to visit. Soon as we do—if we do—we'll head out."

"Yes, sir," said the lieutenant.

The third and final airlift of CIVMARS included a ship's cook, a middle-aged woman with blond hair streaked with gray who set to work inventorying the Franklin's supplies. Her name was Sandra but everyone called her Cookie. That night the Coast Guardsmen had their first real meal in two days. Each of them complimented Cookie, telling her that if MSC crews ate that well, then by god, they were joining the CIVMARS once they retired.

Restoration of electrical power restored the ship's Internet satellite connection, too. After dinner, Gates and Strange researched the Russian rig on their laptops.

Called the Vilanovsky, it was the newest in a class of Russian Arctic-hardened drilling platforms called Offshore

Ice-Resistant Fixed Platforms, or ORIRFP. It was the sister platform to the Prirazolmnaya which operated in the Pechora Sea's Prirazlomnoye oil field. That rig had been plagued by controversy and protests from environmentalists when towed to sea several years earlier. Gazprom, the Russian oil company that owned the Prirazolmnaya, tried to allay fears with a massive public relations program, inviting journalists from around the world to visit the rig. It did little to allay the fears of environmentalists.

A different company, Aelsalon Energy, owned the Vilanovsky. Aelsalon was privately held, which, according to their research, meant the company was owned by undisclosed Russian political interests. Their research also showed the movement and placement of Vilanovsky was done in secret, with no publicity and no invitations for media tours.

"My bet is it will be a no-go for us, too," Gates said.

Gates stood on the fantail of the Franklin, next to the giant A-crane. The CIVMARS had succeeded in deploying an anchor, and, with her bow turned into the sea, the Franklin rode much better. The ship rolled gently. Flowing water hissed softly as it rushed along its sides, joined now and then by the hollow thunk of drift ice banging against the hull.

In the dim light of the Arctic night, the Vilanovsky was a small star on the surface of the sea. It sat close to the maritime boundary between Russian and American waters, well outside the Arctic's normal oil fields. That struck Gates as strange, but since the polar melt every country with an Arctic border was exploring the sea bed for new mineral riches.

"Commander Gates?"

He turned at the voice and found a short, dark-skinned woman holding a coffee mug and insulated pitcher. She was Asian. Or was she Inuit? Gates wasn't sure. Her eyes were large and spaced wide apart. Both her nose and mouth small, but her smile displayed beautiful white teeth set against her reddish-brown complexion. Long, raven-black hair parted in the middle and made up in twin braids fell across each shoulder. She was young and quite pretty.

"My name is Panik Ublureak," she said with a slight accent Gates couldn't place. She laughed at the sound of her own name. "Everyone calls me Nikki. I am the ship's steward. Captain Gunnar thought you might need coffee."

Gates took the proffered cup.

"Thank you," he said. The ceramic mug warmed his hands and steam wafted from its contents. He blew on it, then took a sip. It was hot and strong. "I didn't see you come aboard with the others."

Nikki smiled. "I am small," she said, "among big people. It is easy to miss me."

"Are you from around here," Gates said, realizing how stupid that sounded. "I mean, are you Inuit?"

"My family goes way back," she said. "From here and there. We have been here for a long time."

"Well, thank you for the coffee," he said. "It's delicious."

"You are different than the others," she said. "You see things differently."

"I don't know what you mean."

"You have greater vision," she said. "Where I come, we say you see more than others."

Gates tensed.

"Did Captain Gunnar tell you that?"

"He only told me you are here to solve a mystery," Nikki said. "The mystery of how the people on this ship disappeared."

"Yes, that's true," Gates said, and he sipped more coffee.

"There are many stories of strange things in this area," she said.

"What kind of strange stories?"

Nikki pointed to the star-flecked sky. "They say sometimes the stars change. One will move. Another will fall from the sky. Sometimes, people disappear. Even entire villages."

"Well, there are meteors in the sky," Gates said, "and sometimes they fall to earth as meteorites. And there are satellites, too."

"But you know there is more than that," Nikki said. "More coffee?"

"No," Gates said, uneasy with the discussion. "Thank you."

Nikki smiled, dipped her head, and walked away.

Gates turned to the Vilanovsky again. His mug banged into the A-crane, spilling much of the coffee. Gates cursed, his hand burning from the hot liquid.

"Hey, Nikki." He turned to look for the girl, but she was gone. He trotted across the deck, looked up the starboard air castle, the open walkway that ran the length of the ship, then the port, seeing no one.

How did she disappear so fast?

Gates shrugged, took one last look at the Vilanovsky, then walked to his cabin.

Chapter 10

The Kamov Ka-62 helicopter flared its approach to the Vilanovsky, hovered outboard of the helo pad, side-slipped over it, and settled within the yellow safety circle. The twin-engine, single-rotor Kamov was painted burnt orange, typical of aircraft operating in the Arctic, save for a blue-and-red pinstripe stretching from the bottom of its nose to its multi-bladed rotor in the tail ring. As the whine of the dual turbines quieted, the fuselage door opened and a set of steps dropped into place.

Aleksandr Konstantin, chief executive officer of the Russian energy giant Aelsalon Energy, stepped from the Kamov. Konstantin was approaching seventy and heavy set. A heavy, fur *ushaka* covered his head. The collar of his parka matched the hat's fur, and he turned it up against the Arctic chill as he stooped beneath the still-revolving blades and hurried toward the two men waiting for him. Behind Konstantin, the two pilots emerged from the helicopter, carrying his luggage.

The men waiting for Konstantin were Sergey Novikov, the Vilanovsky's director of operations, and Pyotr Praskovya, chief of security. Praskovya, a tall, dark man with black, gray-flecked hair, stood to Novikov's right and a step or two behind the op's chief. This was in deference to the short, thin, and bespectacled man's position on the Vilanovsky, though the security chief knew full well he carried far more authority over operations than Novikov.

Konstantin greeted Novikov first, grasping his hand and patting the director's shoulders, then turned to the security chief.

"Petya!" he cried, addressing Praskovya with the diminutive of his given name. He embraced the security man in a bear hug, then held him at arm's length. "How long has it been, Petya?"

"Far, far too long, Aleks," Praskovya said. He took Konstantin by the shoulder and led him away from the helicopter platform. "Come, come. We must eat and drink. Afterward, we can brief you on our operations here."

The Vilanovsky, like its sister platform, was a veritable battleship among oil rigs. The platform was 126 square meters—more than 1,300 square feet—and displaced 117,000 tons without ballast. Ballasted, it weighed some 506,000 tons. The operations platform sat on a massive steel caisson designed to withstand the crushing force of Arctic ice. The caisson sat on the ocean floor, secured by its own weight. Its top section still rose many feet above the surface. Perched on the caisson was the intermediate deck, its dark orange walls rising bunker-like above the drift ice. The operations platform and accommodations module sat atop the intermediate deck. Above them stretched an enclosed drilling tower, looking more like a high-rise building than a derrick. Like the tower, all work areas aboard the Vilanovsky were protected against the elements.

Novikov and Praskovya led Konstantin into the enclosed drilling deck, and up a ladder to the accommodations module, which contained berthing for the crew, offices and laboratories, a conference room and canteen, and the platform's control center. Konstantin removed his parka and fur cap, and ran his hand through his thick, white hair. They settled in the conference room where they exchanged small

talk while they lunched on hot cabbage soup and fried pi-
rozhki pies filled with meat and sautéed onions, and washed
down with vodka and Scotch.

A worker came in and cleared away the plates and
glasses, then served spiced coffee.

"Gentlemen, thank you for a meal fit for a tsar," Konstantin said as the servers left. "But now, we must speak
business. Sergey, how much progress have we made?"

The operations director's shoulders sagged.

"I am afraid I must report not much, sir," he mumbled.
He wore narrow, black-rimmed reading glasses which he
adjusted on his nose. "We are still having difficulties with
the equipment."

"Difficulties?" Konstantin said. He turned toward
Praskovya as if seeking confirmation. The security chief
shrugged, then nodded. The CEO turned back to Novikov.
"What difficulties? Please explain."

"Power outages, hydraulic failures, electrical problems," said Novikov. "In the past two months we have had
seventeen complete power outages. The diesel-electric generators—they simply stop working. Our technicians take
them apart and find nothing amiss. They put the generators
together again, and they work—for a few days, at least—
before they stop working again. We've had numerous short
circuits and power surges that knock out our electronics. We
even had one man fatally electrocuted. You saw the report
on that, sir?"

"I did," Konstantin said, nodding. "Go on."

"Our hydraulics stop working," Novikov continued. He
tore the glasses from his face and waved them in frustration.
"They act as if the fluid is frozen in the hoses. Other times
leaks develop in perfectly good pipes and hoses. One of

those leaks resulted in a fire that nearly forced us to abandon the platform. You saw that report, too?"

Konstantin nodded again. "Is it because our domestic equipment is improperly made? We can buy foreign-made products to replace it. This project is too important to stand on nationalism."

"As far as we can tell, our equipment is fine," Novikov said, waving his glasses. "There is no reason we can find for these failures. It is as if . . ." The operations director waved his hands in the air trying to capture the word he needed. "What did our pilots blame equipment problems on during the Great Patriotic War?"

"Gremlins," Praskovya said. "An English word for make-believe creatures who tampered with their aircraft."

"Yes, gremlins," Novikov said, as if satisfied. "As if gremlins are wreaking havoc on our work here."

"I doubt gremlins are your problem, Sergey," Konstantin said. "But other troublemakers?" He turned to Praskovya. "Sabotage, perhaps?"

"Aleks, I had the background of every worker on this platform checked and rechecked for any suspicious activities, or associations with known hooligan groups or environmentalists or other foreigners. I also placed workers under observation when they return to the mainland on their leaves. *Nichego*. Nothing."

"Have you posted guards at vital areas where these failures occurred?" Konstantin asked.

Praskovya shook his head.

"Where would we post them?" he said. "The failures always occur in different parts of the platform among unrelated equipment. My men patrol discreetly among the workers, keeping an eye of them, but have seen nothing suspicious."

"And your own men are trustworthy?" Konstantin asked. "Every one of them?"

"I trust them with my life," Praskovya said. "Have done so on many occasions. I have known each of them for years. They come from where I do."

The security chief glanced sideways at Novikov, but the operations director was busy stirring his coffee.

"Is it the cold?" Konstantin suggested. "Perhaps the cold is affecting the equipment?"

Novikov looked up from his coffee and shook his head.

"No, sir," he said. "Our equipment is rated for the Arctic environment. Most of it is identical to that found on other Arctic drilling platforms. The only difference is . . ."

He let the sentence hang. Konstantin and Praskovya understood his reference and nodded.

"Well," said Konstantin, "we can only continue on. These are mere interruptions. They may slow us, but they cannot defeat us. In light of the extreme circumstance under which you work, you and your people are doing an excellent job, Sergey."

A smile flickered across the director's face. "Thank you, sir."

"Now, if you will leave us. Petya and I have sensitive matters of security to discuss."

"Of course." Novikov pushed back his chair and stood.

"Oh, one thing," Konstantin said. "We had a request from the American State Department. It appears one of their Arctic research vessels has had an incident." He glanced at Praskovya before continuing. "Their Coast Guard is investigating and requests our assistance."

Konstantin looked at Praskovya. The security chief blanched.

"Assistance?" asked Novikov.

"Yes, they want to visit the Vilanovsky and talk to us, to see if we noticed anything unusual."

"Surely, you denied the request," Praskovya said.

"Not at all," Konstantin said. "I agreed. I even offered the use of my helicopter to transport them here."

"But . . ."

Konstantin raised a hand.

"Is it not the rule of the sea that mariners aid those in distress?" Novikov and Praskovya both nodded. "Then it would be suspicious for me not to agree."

"But what if . . ."

Konstantin cut off Novikov again.

"They will come and they will see an ordinary oil drilling operation, Sergey," he said. "One of dozens being activated in the Arctic Ocean since the polar melt by every country with an Arctic border. Nothing more. Now go. Petya and I need to talk."

When the director of operations left, Konstantin turned to Praskovya and sighed.

"Petya, Petya, Petya," he said, "what have you done?"

The security chief took from his pocket a box of Belomorkanal, a brand of *papirose*, or cigarettes, and withdrew one. It had a long cardboard tube topped with a shorter paper tube of tobacco. Praskovya pinched the cardboard tube twice, the crimps perpendicular to each other, then gripped the impromptu cigarette holder with his teeth. He lit it with a battered gasoline lighter, inhaled a lungful of pungent smoke, and started to speak. Konstantin held up his hand.

"I know you believe you did what you had to do," the older man said. "But it has been a long, long time since I was KGB and you were Spetsnaz. We're not young men anymore, Petya,"

Praskovya started to speak again and was once more stopped.

"Simplicity, Petya," Konstantin said. "Today, simplicity is the watch word. We can no longer afford the time and expense of the parlor tricks you so enjoy. We do not want another San Diego incident, do we?"

Praskovya slumped in his seat, thick gray smoke swirling around his head. Praskovya had served in the Russian Navy's elite Spetsnaz, or naval commandos, where he was known as much for his brashness as for his courage and military prowess. The Spetsnaz used tracked, underwater vehicles for reconnaissance. One night while operating from a submarine submerged off the Southern California coast, Praskovya drove such a vehicle straight into San Diego Bay, home to one of the U.S. Navy's greatest concentrations of ships. The next morning, security forces at North Island Naval Air Station discovered tank tracks leading from the water up to the fence line surrounding a nuclear weapons depot. Foot prints led from the tank tracks and along the fence line, then back to the tracks, which led back to the water.

The message they left was clear: We're here. The incident, however, led to a diplomatic brouhaha that lasted for months.

Praskovya straightened in his chair and spoke.

"Aleks, we had to do something when we discovered their miniature submarine near the base of this platform. We needed to know what they knew. So, we captured the submarine and brought it back to our moon pool."

Konstantin nodded. "And you interrogated the occupants to determine what they knew."

"They claimed their compass failed, and they lost their bearings."

"You didn't believe them."

"No."

"So, you killed them."

Praskovya nodded.

"Understandable. But why did you return their submarine to the research ship? Why not sink it and let the ship crew believe there was an accident?"

Praskovya dropped his head in embarrassment and let Konstantin answer his own question.

"Because that is the type of brash act Petya Praskovya is famous for, correct?"

The security chief nodded, still looking at his own boots.

"And the ship itself?" Konstantin asked.

"We had no idea how much the Americans knew about our operations," Praskovya said. "We assaulted at night, captured the crew and interrogated them. They, too, claimed to know nothing. We searched their computers and recording devices, but found nothing related to our operations. To be safe, we used a degausser to erase all data. We disabled the ship in case there was anyone hiding we had not found, placed explosives, and eliminated the crew. If everything had gone well, it would simply have been another lost ship, another mystery of the sea."

"But everything did not go well. Why?"

Praskovya snubbed out his cigarette before answering.

"We were operating under sterile conditions so nothing could be traced back to us or the government. Foreign clothing and weapons . . . and explosives. Our plastic explosives and detonators came from the Balkans. Much of what we get from there is rubbish. Next time we should buy from the Americans."

"Petya," Konstantin said, "Let us hope there will be no need for a next time."

Chapter 11

Gates thought of his father as he and Leland Strange watched the Russian Kamov Ka-62 approach from the northeast. His father, also a career Coast Guardsman, was a Cold War warrior. He fought in the Vietnam war, serving on an 82-foot patrol boat prowling the Vietnamese coast looking for Viet Cong junks smuggling weapons and ammunition into the south. He had served on cutters in the North Atlantic, shadowing Soviet spy ships, and took part in NATO naval maneuvers designed as a show of force against the USSR. Gates and Leland, both dressed in orange survival suits, were waiting for a Russian helicopter to ferry them to a Russian oil platform. What was it his father always said about U.S. relations with Russia after the collapse of the Soviet Union? "My how things have changed."

Maybe things hadn't really changed, Gates told himself.

"Leland," he said, leaning closer to the lieutenant to be heard over the roar of the approaching aircraft's engines, "remember not to let on you speak Russian, okay?"

"Yes, sir," Strange said.

The Kamov side-slipped across the helo pad and settled in the middle of its safety ring. A minute later, the fuselage door opened and the stairs unfolded. A man in a survival suit stepped onto the deck and trotted over to them.

"Commander Gates?" he said in heavily accented English.

"I'm Gates."

The man smiled, showing large, tobacco-stained teeth, and held out his hand. Gates shook it.

"My name is Sukelov, second pilot for Mr. Konstantin's helicopter," he said. "I have the pleasure of extending Mr. Konstantin's invitation to join us on the Vilanovsky."

"Thank you," Gates said, turning toward Leland. "This is Lieutenant Strange, my second in command."

Sukelov shook Strange's hand, then urged the two men toward the helicopter.

"Come, please. Mr. Konstantin awaits your arrival."

They flew low and fast over the drift ice, the first pilot at the controls as Sukelov maintained a constant dialog with the Americans, eager to practice his English while he could. As they approached the oil platform, what had been a speck of light on the far horizon became a towering behemoth in the isolated sea. Strange stared out the window at the platform, the eyes behind the eyeglasses capturing details Gates knew he himself would never notice. Attention to detail, Gates thought, is how you get a Ph.D. in your early twenties.

The helicopter settled on the oil platform, and its turbines spun down, their whine growing softer. Sukelov opened the door, dropped the stairs, then stood aside.

"Welcome aboard the Vilanovsky," he said. "Enjoy your visit, gentlemen."

Three men waited for them at the edge of the helo pad. One was bound in a fur-lined parka and matching fur cap. Another was tall and thin, with dark hair and glasses. He, too, wore a parka and hat against the chill. The third man was tall, well-built, with short, gray-flecked hair. He wore only a light jacket and appeared not to mind the cold. Gates took special notice of him.

Konstantin stepped forward, hand out toward Gates.

"Commander Gates," he said. It wasn't a question. "Welcome to the Vilanovsky. My name is Aleksandr Konstantin, chief executive officer of Aelsalon Energy."

Gates shook the Russian's hand, noting his perfect English.

"Commander Douglas Gates, U.S. Coast Guard, sir. Thank you for accommodating us." He turned toward Strange. "Lieutenant Leland Strange, my executive officer."

Konstantin shook Leland's hand, then turned to Gates.

"Are our military men getting younger every year, or am I just getting older?" he said, smiling. He inserted himself between the Americans and led them to the two other men. "Come. Allow me to introduce Sergey Novikov, my director of operations, and Pyotr Praskovya, my chief of security."

The four men shook hands. Gates eyed Praskovya, then asked, "Chief of security?"

"For protection from environmentalist hooligans," Konstantin said. "Such people repeatedly attacked our sister platform, the Prirazlomnaya. They boarded the platform in violation of international law. Pure piracy! But I need not tell you of these actions. Your own oil platforms have endured such attacks, have they not?"

"They have, sir," Gates said, thinking more of the Iraqi insurgent attacks on the platform in the Gulf than of environmentalists.

"Come," Konstantin said, "let's go inside. I am sure you will be much more comfortable once you remove those survival suits. Have you ever been on an oil drilling platform, commander?"

"No, sir," Gates said, and cast a wary eye toward Strange. The young officer echoed his senior officer.

71

The Russians led Gates and Strange into the cavernous drilling deck. It spanned the entire width and breadth of the caisson. Towering above the deck was the enclosed derrick and its web of pipes, hoses, cables, and supports. One formidable piece of machinery—the drill, Gates guessed—stabbed into the icy water below. Removable grating formed the deck and surrounded the drill. A quarter of the space was given over to a moon pool, an opening in the deck that provided access to the Arctic water beneath the platform. An overhead bridge crane sat above the moon pool, its block and tackle tangling from one end of its trolley. Three small deep-diving mini-subs sat in cradles on the deck surrounding the moon pool. Hanging on the bulkhead were four atmospheric deep-sea diving suits, bulky hardshell anthropomorphic submersibles with spacesuit-like helmets and articulated legs and arms, the latter ending in pincers.

"You have a lot of deep-diving equipment, Mr. Konstantin," Gates said. "Is that normal for an oil rig?"

"Despite what those environmentalist hooligans say," answered Praskovya, speaking for the first time, "we do our best to protect the environment." His voice was deep, confident. "We have these submersibles so we can do proper maintenance on the well head. And in the event of a problem—say a leak, as improbable as that is—we can respond promptly with a repair party. We do not want to repeat the disaster that occurred in your own waters with the Deepwater Horizons platform. You can understand that."

Gates knew the Deepwater Horizon disaster too well. The ultra-deep-water drilling rig operated in U.S. waters in the Gulf of Mexico. In 2010, it suffered an uncontrollable blowout at the wellhead, five thousand feet deep, which caused an explosion, killing eleven workers and sinking the

Horizon. The lack of deep-diving capabilities hindered efforts to cap the wellhead, leaving oil gushing from the well for months and creating the largest oil spill in history. Gates was among the thousands of Coast Guard personnel who responded to the spill.

"Very responsible of you," Gates said.

Strange bumped Gates and nodded at a stanchion on which sat a square metal box with a glass face. Inside the box was a lever. Large red Cyrillic letters on a yellow background screamed something in Russian.

"It says, 'Emergency Evacuation Alarm,'" Strange whispered. "Maybe they're not as confident as they claim to be."

They crossed the drilling deck, climbed metal stairs to the accommodations module, and entered. The instant change of temperature made Gates and Strange sweat.

"Please, gentlemen," Konstantin said, "you can remove your outer garments and leave them here." He opened the door to a locker, which held several similar survival suits.

Once relieved of their survival suits, Konstantin led them through a hallway lined by offices and labs. Gates followed, with Strange and Novikov behind him. Praskovya, the security man, came last. Leland turned to the operations director and asked, "How are your drilling operations proceeding, Mr. Novikov?"

Novikov, surprised at being addressed by the American, brightened.

"Oh, well," he said. "Quite well. Aside from minor trouble from Kremlins."

Everyone stopped and looked at Novikov.

"Kremlins?" asked Gates.

Praskovya snapped a quick bark at Novikov in Russian, then said, "He means gremlins. Novikov's English is not so good."

"Yes, yes," Novikov said, embarrassed. "Gremlins. Little trouble makers, yes?"

The security chief barked again in Russian. Konstantin chuckled.

"Yes, there are always gremlins in the works, no matter what you do," he said. "Don't you agree, commander?"

Gates agreed, then commented, "Speaking of English, Mr. Konstantin, yours is very good. I could mistake you for an American."

"And why not?" the Russian said, with a laugh as he showed them into the conference room. "I spent many years in your country."

"Business?" Leland asked.

"Of a kind," Konstantin said. "I was KGB."

The Russian laughed at the expression on the Americans' faces.

"Come, come, gentlemen," he said. "That was a lifetime ago. When the old Soviet Union came to an end, so did my allegiance to communism. I became a dedicated capitalist." He stopped, smiled, and raised a finger. "Though some might say there is not much difference between the two. Perhaps the only changes are the people you must bribe to get things done."

Gates sensed an uncomfortable stiffness in both Praskovya and Novikov and changed the subject.

"Your English is good, too, Mr. Praskovya," he said. "KGB, too?"

"*Nyet*," Praskovya said. "That is, no. As with you, I was a humble naval officer. But that, too, was a lifetime ago."

"Gentlemen, shall we come to the business you came here for?" Konstantin said. "Your state department said you wanted to know if we knew or saw anything unusual regarding this research ship Franklin, correct?"

"Yes, sir," Gates said.

Konstantin gestured toward a set of binders.

"These are our rough and finished logbooks," he said. "Petya has read through them. He will brief you on his findings. Meanwhile, I will order us coffee."

As Konstantin left, Praskovya picked up a binder, turned to a page marker, and skimmed the page.

"Our first encounter with this Franklin was four weeks ago," he said. "She was operating to the east of us. As you know, the Vilanovsky sits close to the Russian-U.S. maritime boundary. At one point, she came within hailing distance and we exchanged casual greetings, as passing ships do."

Praskovya turned to another marked page, and skimmed it, too.

"Ah, yes," he said. "This second interchange occurred on July 4." He looked up. "Your Independence Day. The Franklin was now to the southwest of us. At approximately 2300 hours, our watch standers in Main Control noticed what appeared to be flares at several miles distance. Thinking they were from a ship in distress, they sent out a general radio hail to whatever party was in distress." Praskovya looked up and chuckled. "A party is what it turned out to be. The Franklin was celebrating your holiday by setting off fireworks. Our people wished them a happy holiday and promised to raise a toast to American independence when they were off duty."

Praskovya closed the logbook and set it back onto the table.

"That was our last communication with them," he said. "Other than a distant light on the horizon, we never saw or heard from them again."

"That was almost a week before the Franklin disappeared," Gates said. "Five days later our search planes found her abandoned."

"Abandoned?" Konstantin said, returning with a canteen worker carrying a tray of cups, saucers, and a coffee carafe.

"It appears so, sir," Gates said. "The ship's single life boat was missing, with no sign of life on board."

The canteen worker set the tray on the table and left. Konstantin picked up a cup and the carafe.

"A true sea mystery," he said. "Coffee?"

He poured cups for everyone as Gates continued.

"Let me ask you, Mr. Praskovya," he said, "as security chief, have you any knowledge or received any reports of piracy in these waters?"

"Piracy? Why no." Praskovya looked surprised at the question, but a moment later his expression changed. "No, wait. I seem to remember a report that came to us a while ago about unusual ship movements in these waters. I assumed they were more of these environmental protesters. Do you remember that report, Aleks?"

Konstantin's face showed brief surprise, but then he said, "Yes. Yes, I believe I do." He waved his hand in dismissal. "Hooligans. More of that hooligan nonsense."

Lieutenant Strange finished his coffee and placed the empty cup in its saucer.

"Delicious coffee," he said. "I wonder if I could bother you for directions to the . . ."

"Of course," said Konstantin. "Out the door to the left." He held up his thumb and forefinger. "The door with the little figure of a man."

Leland found the restroom. As with most Russian public restrooms, privacy was not considered in its design. A tight row of three toilets stood against one bulkhead with nothing between them but paper dispensers and waste canisters. A row of closely placed urinals afforded the same degree of privacy.

As he finished using a urinal, two Russian workers came in, speaking in loud, angry voices. They halted and stared at the American as he faced them. One of them said something to him in Russian. Leland pretended not to understand.

"I'm sorry. I don't understand Russian," he said.

The Russian looked perplexed a moment, then smiled. "Amerikanski?"

Leland nodded.

The Russian turned to his companion. "Amerikanski!" He turned back to Leland and said in slow, accented English, "They . . . tell us . . . you visit. Welcome to Vilanovsky!"

Both men patted Leland on the back and shoulders, then stepped up to the urinals. Leland slipped out of the restroom and took his time returning to the meeting, peeking through windows into offices and laboratories. One lab had a large whiteboard covered with Cyrillic writing except for one word written in large, capital Latin alphabet letters.

"Ah, Lieutenant Strange. We thought you might be lost."

Praskovya hurried toward him.

"Ah, no, sir, not lost," Strange said. "I made friends with two of your workers in the restroom. They were welcoming me aboard. At least, I think they were. Then this laboratory caught my attention. Oceanographic lab, isn't it? I'm an oceanographer by training."

"Yes, yes, it is," the security chief said. He guided Leland toward the conference room. "However, our oceanographer is ashore today. I'm sure he would have enjoyed talking . . . shop . . . with you. That is how you say it?"

After the Americans left, Konstantin and Praskovya sat around the conference table, finishing their coffee. Praskovya drew a cigarette from a pack of Belomokanals, pinched its cardboard tube, and lit it.

"Well, what do you think, Petya?"

Praskovya blew smoke rings as he considered his answer.

"It went better than I feared, Aleks," he said. "We had limited official contact with the research ship. They could have questioned the crew and received the same story as from the logbook."

"That was quick thinking when the commander asked about pirates," Konstantin. "Of course, there was no such report?"

Praskovya shook his head, smoke snaking around his head as he exhaled. "No," he said, "but it was a viable pretense for misdirection. With luck they will conclude pirates attacked the research ship. And thank you for realizing my little charade so swiftly."

"And the young black officer?" Konstantin said. "You found him looking into the oceanography lab?"

"Yes, he said he was trained as an oceanographer."

"You believed him?"

Praskovya shrugged. "It is possible."

"That was a lapse in security, Petya, having our laboratory visible to our visitors," Konstantin said. "Perhaps he saw something?"

"Relax, Aleks," Praskovya said. "I found and interviewed the two workers who accosted him in the lavatory, and they said it was clear he did not understand a word they said. There was nothing he could see in the laboratory he would understand unless he spoke Russian."

"Still," said Konstantin, standing, "it was a lapse of security, one that will not be countenanced again."

Konstantin walked out, leaving Praskovya bathed in a cloud of smoke.

Chapter 12

W ell, gentlemen, welcome back. How did your meeting with the Rooskis go?"

Captain Gunnar pulled a chair out from the conference table and sat across from Gates. Leland Strange sat at the end of the table, focused on his laptop.

"They were gracious hosts," Gates said, "until Leland got caught peeking through a window into a laboratory. They remained friendly, but they gave us something of a bum's rush exit."

"Learn anything?"

Gates grunted. "Not much," he said. "They exchanged radio greetings once as the Franklin steamed past, then again on July 4. After that, nothing. At least that's what they told us."

"We learned more than that, commander," Strange said, looking up from the computer. "When I was in the head, two workers came in. They were angry, something about more equipment failures. One of them thought the Vilanovsky was jinxed. But the other said—and I'm quoting here—'It's not jinxed. It's because of that thing below.'"

"What thing below?"

"I don't know, sir. Once they saw me, they stopped talking and welcomed me aboard."

"What about that lab Praskovya caught you looking into?" Gates asked.

"That was interesting, too," Strange said. "There was a whiteboard with notes about energy emissions and measurements."

"Energy emissions?" Gates said. "What kind?"

"They're trying to that figure out. They were taking measurements of an unknown energy source on the ocean floor. Several types of emissions, electromagnetic, thermal . . ."

Strange paused, his brow knitting.

"Even gravitational. Some forms they couldn't classify." Strange shrugged. "What was interesting was that most of the notes were written in the Cyrillic alphabet as you'd expect on a Russian rig. But there was one word written in our alphabet, in very large capital letters and underlined three times. I don't know what the word means. It was o-o-p-a-r-t. Oopart?"

"You're sure?" Gates asked.

"Yes, sir," Strange said. "Do you know it, commander?"

Gates nodded. "It's an archeology term, an acronym for out-of-place artifact."

"What does 'out-of-place artifact' mean, Doug?" Gunnar asked.

"It refers to finding an example of a technology more advanced than expected in the remains of the culture you're studying," Gates explained. "A famous example is the Antikythera Mechanism, a very advanced form of mechanical computer found in a Greek shipwreck from around 150 B.C.E."

"Oh, I've read about that," Leland said. "It was an astronomical computer, wasn't it?"

"So, it's believed," Gates said. "Another OOPART is the Piri Reis chart."

"That's one I've heard of," said Gunnar. He stroked his beard, remembering. "Read about it a maritime magazine. It's supposed to show the coastline of the Antarctic continent without the ice cover. It was drawn by an ancient Turkish admiral, right?"

"That's right, captain," Gates said. "Piri Reis was a Turkish admiral and cartographer who lived in the 1500s. He drew the chart, but he said he used several earlier charts as source material. What's remarkable is how accurately it depicts Antarctica's coastline without its ice coverage, which existed long before man. We didn't have any idea what the land mass beneath the ice looked like until radar came along in the 20th century."

"Wasn't there something about the ancient Egyptians having electricity?" Strange asked.

"Even before the Egyptians," Gates said. "The Sumerians in ancient Mesopotamia. Researchers found clay jars with metal electrodes. They found if you filled the jars with wine or vinegar, they produced a small electrical current. For lack of a better name, they're called the Baghdad Batteries, though that's a misnomer. Most researchers believe they were used for electroplating rather than generating electricity."

Gates tapped his fingers on the table, thinking.

"In what you read on that whiteboard, Leland, did they have any idea whether this energy source was technological or natural?" he said.

"I don't think they knew," Strange said. "But if I were to make an educated guess, the fact they used the English term OOPART indicates they thought it might be technological."

Gunnar scoffed. "Are you suggesting the Russians may have found the lost city of Atlantis, lieutenant?"

"I am simply making a suggestion based on what I read, captain," Strange said.

Gunnar held up his hand. "Just kidding, lieutenant," he said. "Just a small joke. Too small, I guess."

"What I don't get is why the Vilanovsky?" Gates said. "If the Russians found a new energy source that's not petroleum, why plant a massive oil drilling platform over it? Why not use a research ship like the Franklin?"

"That's one other thing we've learned, sir," Strange said. He spun the laptop around so Gates and Gunnar could see the screen. "I told you I spent time on Russian oil rigs when I was studying in Russia. There were things aboard the Vilanovsky that struck me as odd. First, the drill didn't look right. It didn't look like the others I've seen. Now, it's a new platform. It could be a form of new drilling technology." Leland shrugged. "And the moon pool and all those submersibles. I've never seen that on other oil platforms. Usually, they use remotely operated vehicles to maintain the drill head. Safer than sending a diver down. And then there's this."

He tapped the computer screen. It showed an aerial photo of the Prirazlomnaya platform.

"This is the Vilanovsky's sister platform," Strange continued. "They look identical right?"

Gates nodded.

"Except for these." Strange pointed to two large cranes angling out from opposite corners of the platform. "This platform has fourteen storage tanks for the crude oil they suck up. They store the crude in those tanks until oil tankers come to collect it, then transfer it to the tankers through large hoses. These cranes lift and maneuver the hoses into place on board the tankers."

Leland paused and turned to Gates.

"Commander, when we were on the Vilanovsky, did you see any large cranes?"

Gates thought back to their approach to the platform. "No, I didn't," he said.

"Nor did I," Strange said. "So, if the Vilanovsky is drilling for oil, what do they do with it after they find it?"

"Good question, Leland," Gates, sitting back in his chair. After a moment, he turned to the CIVMAR captain. "Any success in the engine room?

"None," Gunnar said, frowning. "Jerry Weil and your Senior Chief Hopper have torn the main motor and generator apart and put it together again, and it still doesn't work. They've been tearing that engine room apart looking for a cause, but nothing."

Strange, his focus still on the laptop, muttered, "Kremlins."

Gunnar looked at the young officer. "What's that?"

Gates grinned and explained.

"The ops director on the Vilanovsky said they were having equipment failures. He blamed them on gremlins, but he mispronounced it."

Gunnar and Gates chuckled, but Strange looked up, his face serious.

"No, I mean it, sirs," he said. "Remember the worker in the men's head complaining about those failures? He blamed them on what he called 'that thing below.' Maybe this energy source *is* the source of their equipment failures, and maybe it's also affecting the Franklin."

"But only our main propulsion? Not the auxiliary generators?" Gates said.

Strange shrugged. "Perhaps it has something to do with proximity or wattage output?"

"Gremlins didn't tear the wiring out of that power panel," Gates said.

"Well, whatever," Gunnar said, his tone expressing doubt. "Gremlins or not, in four days it won't matter. I got a message today. That damaged oil rig I mentioned yesterday? One of the tugs was released and is en route to take us under tow. It should be here in three or four days."

A rap came at the door, and Senior Chief Hopper stepped inside.

"Excuse me, sirs," he said, then addressed Gates. "Skipper, Jess and Frank found something below decks you should see."

"What, senior chief?"

Hopper shook his head, rolled chaw around, then spit into his ever-present soda can.

"I really think you need to see this, sir."

Gates and Strange rose to follow Hopper out of the room when Gunnar asked, "Mind if I join you, Doug?"

"Of course, captain."

As they left the compartment, Strange took Gates aside and whispered, "Sir, that chewing tobacco habit of the senior chief's is not only unhealthy—he can get mouth cancer from it—it's disgusting, too. Can't you order him to not indulge when he's around others?"

Gates prodded the younger officer on.

"Leland, there are some things man has no control over," he said. "Time, tide, and senior chief's chaw."

They followed the senior chief down ladders until they reached the third deck, where Brown and Chee waited. Frank Chee, a helicopter rescue swimmer and team medic, was a strongly built Navajo who had never seen an ocean until joining the Coast Guard. Still, he turned out to be a powerful swimmer with no fear of heights or rough water, the perfect candidate for the tough and dangerous job of air-survival man, those Coasties trained to jump out of helicopters into storm-tossed seas to pull drowning mariners to safety.

Chee and Brown stood in the central passageway next to a firefighting station. The emergency station had a red platform the size and shape of a folding poker table mounted vertically on the bulkhead, two feet above the deck. The stand held a coiled fire hose with an all-purpose nozzle. The hose was attached to a nearby high-pressure water valve. To the right of the stand were a fire ax and CO_2 extinguisher.

"What have you got?" Gates asked.

"Well, sir, something about this passageway bothered Frank and me since we searched the ship for more explosives," Brown said. "You see, sir, these two storage compartments—" He pointed to two doors on either side of the firefighting station. "They didn't seem right. The square footage didn't add up. It kept bothering us. While you and the L-T were gone, Frank and I came down here and sounded the bulkheads." He held up a small hammer used for tapping the metal walls of a ship. "And we found a hollow."

"They didn't know you and the lieutenant were back aboard, sir." Hopper said. "So, they reported this to me."

Hopper nodded to Chee. The team medic reached behind the rim of the stand. There was a click, then Chee pulled on the platform's edge. It swung open, revealing a hatchway leading into a slim compartment. Shelves crowded with electronic equipment lined each bulkhead, leaving enough room for a single chair. The chair was se-cured with bungee cords to the far bulkhead.

Chee's dark, chiseled face broke into a boyish grin.

"Pretty cool, huh, skipper?"

The two officers looked at each other.

"Well," said Gates, "this has been an interesting day."

Chapter 13

N o doubt about it, commander, the Franklin is a spy ship."

Georgia Stalk sat in the tight confines of the hidden compartment, running her hand over the various instruments. She had been working in one of the ship's labs, trying to recover data from the erased computers, when Gates called her down to the third deck and the tiny hidden room.

"Everything here is what you'd find on any naval spy ship for collecting signals and electronic intelligence—only miniaturized." Stalk pointed to a device. "This is an acoustic receiver, passive sonar used for collecting underwater sounds—submarine noises and such—for analysis and identification. There must be a microphone array on the bottom of the hull or in a pod. Or maybe an automated towed array."

Stalk touched another display, then another, explaining each one. "Scanning radio receiver. When it hits a busy freq, it starts recording. Electronic emissions detector—radar, infrared, and such. Radiation detector; unusual but not unheard of. It's fully automated. Whatever it sniffs out, it records and burst transmits it via satellite to—well, wherever."

"You're certain of that, chief?" Gates said. "This couldn't be oceanographic equipment?"

"I'm certain as rain, sir," Stalk said. "It's standard equipment for an intelligence ship. But my favorite young lieutenant is standing next to you, and he's a famous ocean-ographer." The chief gave Strange a motherly smile. "Ask him."

Gates looked at Strange. "Leland?"

The young man shook his head. "I've never seen equipment like this used for oceanography before, sir," he said. "Well, except for the acoustic receiver. Since the end of the Cold War, researchers have used the Navy's old SOSUS sound surveillance systems to study whale sounds. But the Franklin has—or had—several oceanographers on board. They'd want the data in their hands right away. Why send it out unseen? I agree with Chief Stalk, sir. This is a spy ship."

Gates and Strange turned to Gunnar.

"Don't look at me," Gunnar protested. "All I was told was to come out and fetch the damn ship home."

Gates leaned against the bulkhead and ran both hands through his dark, close-cropped hair.

"Well, we can conclude whatever happened to the crew of the Franklin had something to do to this compartment," he said. "And why the computers in the labs were erased."

"And bombs planted to sink the ship," Leland said.

Gates nodded.

"At some point, the Franklin must have gotten close enough to record something that somebody didn't want recorded," he said. "Since there aren't that many somebodies in this part of the Arctic . . ."

"The Vilanovsky," Strange said.

"I wish I could get another close look at that platform," Gates said, nodding. "Unless a submarine surfaced along-side the Franklin and boarded her, the only suspect left is the Vilanovsky."

"That's impossible, sir," Strange said. "I don't think they'll offer us another invitation. And it's not like we can run a RHIB over there and shout, 'This is the U.S. Coast Guard. Standby to be boarded.'"

"I know, Leland," Gates said. "I know."

"Well," said Gunnar, stroking his beard. There was a glint in the man's gray eyes. "There is one way."

"What's that?" Gates asked.

"You mentioned it a moment ago," Gunnar said.

He waited for Gates to catch on, but the officer's face was blank.

"You go by submarine," Gunnar said.

"This is the Chukchi Sea," said Leland Strange, pointing to a chart of the Arctic Ocean, "north of the Bering Strait. We're here, southwest of Herald Island and its big brother, Wrangel Island. The international sea boundary comes through the Bering Strait, doglegs to the north, then doglegs again to the left, leaving those two islands in Russian waters. Vilanovsky is located here, south of Herald Island, only a couple miles on the other side of the international maritime boundary. There's less than five miles separating us from the platform."

"Can Chip go five miles, Sarah?"

"With no problem," Sandford said. "It'll take a while. Chip was built for deep diving, not speed."

"What's the ocean depth in these waters?" Gates asked.

"We're in luck there, sir, because the Chukchi is the shallowest sea in the Arctic Ocean, only around 50 meters deep—a hundred and fifty feet."

"How deep can Chip go, Sarah?" Gates asked.

"A lot deeper than that, commander," she said. "That's why it's called a *deep* submergence vehicle." She gave

Gates a *what-hell-do-you-think?* smile. She saw Gates blush, apparently embarrassed by his own question. Sarah cleared her throat, regretting the embarrassment she caused him. "We should have no problem, commander."

"I understand the DSV made several dives to the ocean floor before the Franklin went missing," Gunnar said.

"Yes, sir," Sandford said. "That's correct."

They spent much of the night discussing Gunnar's proposal, pouring over charts, debating approaches to the platform, and the risks and benefits of the plan. Later, when everyone else had turned in, Gates stood on the starboard bridge wing and stared across the ice-encrusted sea to the distant light that was the Vilanovsky. To the west, the midnight sun hung low over the horizon. Its light cast shadows across the drift ice. He gnawed at his lower lip, thinking.

What the hell am I getting myself into? he wondered. Sneak across an international boundary line in a tiny submarine to spy on a Russian oil platform? Who the hell did he think he was, Tom Clancy? Still, his mission was to discover what happened to the Franklin crew, and whether whatever caused it still posed a threat to maritime traffic. It wasn't the first time since joining DSF–Papa that he had discovered the unthinkable and had done the unthinkable to neutralize it. His father's voice echoed inside his head with the Coast Guard's unofficial motto, one left over from the days of the U.S. Lifesaving Service: "You have to go out. You don't have to come back."

Yeah, he thought, but the other person I'll be with isn't a Coastie. Sarah Sandford's face came to him with that sensual smile and, despite the risks, he found an odd excitement rising within him at the prospect of being with her alone in the mini-sub. He shook that from his head and concentrated again on the Vilanovsky.

"Commander?"

Gates turned and found the ship's steward grinning at him. The dim sunlight reflected in her large almond eyes. What was her name? Something Inuit. Something unpronounceable. Panik Ublureak. Nikki.

"Nikki," he said in greeting. "What keeps you up so late?"

"Oh, I love to be outside at night and watch the stars as they fall. Do you remember what I told you of my people's stories?"

"How the stars fell from the sky and landed on Earth?"

Nikki nodded, pleased he remembered. "There goes one now!"

Gates looked to the sky and saw the last flicker of a meteor. He chuckled in wonderment.

"How's that for timing?" he said. "You mention falling stars, and suddenly one shows up."

"We know these things," Nikki said. "We know many things others don't. Just as you see things your people don't. We are alike, Commander Gates. You and me and my people."

Gates stiffened again at her remark alluding to his alleged second sight.

"You will be leaving us tomorrow?" Nikki said. "Only for a short time?"

"How did you know?"

"A ship's steward hears many things," she said with a slight giggle.

"Well, we might not go," he said. "The more I think about it . . ."

"You will go," Nikki said. "You must go. And you will find what you need. At least, in part. An answer to one of your questions."

Before Gates could ask Nikki what she meant, the young girl pointed to the sky behind him.

"Another will appear there," she said.

Gates followed her finger. Seconds later, a fiery ember darted through the night and disappeared.

"How do you do that?" he said, turning back to Nikki.

She wasn't there. He looked along the deck and inside the bridge, but the pretty young girl with the unpronounceable name was gone.

"Are you certain you want to go through with this, captain?" Gates asked.

It was morning. Gates, Strange, and Gunnar stood next to the DSV beneath the giant A-frame crane. Sarah Sandford stood atop it, connecting the crane's cables to the sub's lifting points.

"The crew of the Franklin were fellow mariners, Doug," Gunnar said. "I knew her captain from the maritime academy. If the Russians were involved with their disappearance, I want to know about it."

"Understood, sir," Gates said. "But what about Sarah? This might put her in great danger."

"I can take care of myself, commander," Sandford said from Chip's deck. "Thank you for your consideration, but I feel the same way as the captain. The Franklin's two DSV pilots were close friends of mine."

Sandford sat on the edge of Chip's deck, legs dangling over the side. She leaned over, arms resting on her knees, and studied Gates.

"Now, commander, if you prefer not to go, that's fine with me," she said. "I understand how some men feel about women drivers. I can do this on my own. Or . . ." She glanced at Strange with a mischievous smile. "Perhaps I should take the young lieutenant."

Strange's face lit up. "Can I, sir?".

"No, you cannot," Gates said. "I'm going. That is if Ms. Sandford will have me as her passenger."

Sandford jumped to her feet and extended an inviting hand toward the hatch.

"What are we waiting for?" she said.

Gates climbed onto the mini-sub, leaving behind a crestfallen Leland Strange. He turned, snapped a salute to Captain Gunnar, and smiled. "Permission to leave the ship, sir?"

Gunnar grinned and returned the salute. "Permission granted."

"Leland," he said. "You have the conn. You're in command of the team."

The young officer brightened, snapped to attention, and saluted.

"Aye, aye, sir," he said. "Good luck."

Gates waited for Sandford to climb into the DSV. She paused, one leg resting in the open hatch.

"You remembered to dress warmly, didn't you, commander?" she said. "It gets mighty cold down there, and I'm not a cuddler."

Gates climbed into the hatch after Sandford. Gerry Salcedo, Gunnar's chief mate, stood ready at the A-frame's controls. After a signal from Sandford, he lifted Chip from its cradle and slowly swung it out over the stern.

☼

Through the bubble canopy, Gates watched as Gunnar and Strange grew smaller as Chip rose between the legs of the crane. Leland, seeing Gates through the thick Plexiglas, waved. The deck slipped beneath them, replaced by the ocean's shattered white shroud. Two members of the CIVMAR crew steadied the vehicle with painter lines as Salcedo lowered the craft.

"Better brace yourself, commander," Sarah said. "Sometimes these things hit the water hard."

Gates braced himself, but Chip settled softly into the water. Drift ice cracked and scraped around the hull with the sound of ice in a bathtub.

"We're lucky," Sandford said. "Gerry's a good crane operator."

Two CIVMARs, dressed in orange survival suits, approached in a RHIB, disconnected the painters and the crane cables, then backed off.

"Time to button up," commander," Sandford said. "Could you close the hatch?"

Gates nodded and rose from his position.

"And don't forget to dog it," Sandford said, glancing sideways at him with another devilish grin.

Gates gave her a "what-kind-of-idiot-do-you-think-I-am?" look, closed the hatch, and secured the dogging wheel.

Air bubbles erupted from beneath the little sub as its ballast tanks expelled air and took in seawater. The bubbles obscured the view from the canopy. When they cleared, there was only water.

Chapter 14

The view was incredible.

Above them, Gates watched the bottom of the sunlit surface ice drift by, like billowing white clouds. Below them, the water was as dark as a desert sky on a cloudy, moonless night. Gates felt as if he were falling through a limitless universe, enveloped by a thick blanket of darkness, alone in the world.

"Earth to Commander Gates."

Gates turned from the view outside and found Sarah Sandford watching him, chuckling at his boy-like wonder. She sat in the pilot's seat, hands resting lightly on two joysticks, which Gates assumed controlled the sub's movement. In front of her, embedded in the control console, sat a computer screen, in the center of which was a two-dimensional rendering of Chip and its various components.

At the top of the screen, digital readouts displayed dive time, depth in meters, carbon dioxide levels, and battery charge. To the right of Chip's image was a compass rose showing the little submarine's heading. Above the compass image was a digital readout of the compass heading; the reciprocal, or reverse, course was displayed below the compass.

To the left of the DSV image, more digital readouts showed distance to the ocean floor, attitude in the water, horizontal and vertical speed, internal and external temperature and pressure. Touch-screen buttons to the side switched the display to readouts for life support, batteries, propulsion, inertial navigation, cabin lighting, and external lighting.

"Since this is your first time in a DSV," she said, "you should become familiar with the equipment."

Gates pointed out the displays he understood. "Compass heading, depth, yaw and pitch," he said, as if trying to impress Sandford.

"Very good," Sandford said, her voice that of a tolerant school teacher. She tapped the screen button marked Propulsion. The displayed switched to readouts for hydrogen and oxygen levels, temperature, and energy output, and a schematic Gates didn't understand.

"Chip uses a new air-independent propulsion system similar to but much smaller than those used in the latest German U-boats. It's based on fuel-cell technology."

"Like those used in cars today?" Gates said.

Sandford nodded. "Very similar. We have a tank of hydrogen and, because we're underwater, a tank of liquid oxygen. You mix the two and it creates water and electricity."

"Sounds like the Walter submarine," Gates said. He referred to experimental submarines designed by the German engineer Hellmuth Walter near the end of World War II that used hydrogen peroxide and a catalyst to create heat and steam to turn a turbine. With oxygen as a byproduct, the Walter submarine had the potential to operate submerged for weeks.

Sandford turned and gave Gates an approving look.

"Well, I'm impressed, commander," she said. Returning to the controls, she continued. "The Walter engine was based on similar concepts, but it wasn't fuel-cell technology as we know it today. We have the usual batteries, too. The AIP gives us a good cruising speed, but the batteries can give us an extra burst of speed if we need it, or that extra *oomf* if we have to lift something to the surface."

"Oomf? Is that a submariners' term?" Gates said.

"Funny," Sandford said. "Now pay attention." She switched on another screen. Its bifurcated view showed what Gates knew were side-scan sonar images. Sandford touched the image in the lower part of the screen. "Side-scanning sonar gives us views of the ocean floor to port and starboard." She pointed to the upper view. "And forward-looking sonar shows us what's ahead of us so we don't run into a cliff wall or something. These are our eyes down here. There's nothing to see until we reach the sea floor, where the lights become effective."

Sandford pressed the button labeled INERTIAL NAV, and the displayed changed to digital nautical charts showing the current and previous positions of the DSV.

"We can't receive GPS signals submerged," Sandford said, "so we rely on an inertial guidance system the same as our nuke subs. It records our movement through the water."

"Did it record the DSV's movements when it disappeared?"

"No," she said. "First thing I checked when I got it powered up. The memory was erased."

"Same as the Franklin's computers," Gates said. After a moment, he added, "This seems pretty advanced stuff for a research mini-sub."

Sandford's lips formed a sly smile.

"The Chips were built by the Navy to use as a test platform for new technologies," she said. "Oceanographic institutes and the Navy have a reciprocal agreement. The Navy provides the research ships. In return, the institutes perform research for the Navy, some of it classified. Robert Ballard found the Titanic using equipment designed for the Navy.

Before he could use it, though, he used it to complete a couple secret survey missions for the Navy. This DSV and the Franklin were provided under the same kind of agreement." She added *sotto voce*, "But you didn't hear that from me."

"Chip-1, Franklin."

Gerry Salcedo's disembodied voice came from a speaker in the console before Sandford. She grabbed the microphone and replied.

"Franklin, Chip-1. All systems nominal. Descending."

"Gertrude?" Gates asked.

Sandford swung around, her lips parting in a look of surprise.

"Well, commander, you surprise me again," she said. "Yes, the UQC AN/WQC-2 underwater telephone. AKA Gertrude. And here I thought you knew nothing about submarines."

"Submarines need someone to talk to, and surface ships have Gertrudes, too," he said. "And I've been on many surface ships over the years."

Sandford turned back to her displays and played with the joysticks. Gates watched the compass swing around to north-northwest, a course that aimed them directly at the Vilanovsky.

"Franklin, Chip-1," Sandford said into the mic. "Coming to course zero-zero-five degrees. Depth one-five meters. Still descending."

"I once read submarines fly through the water, similar to the way airplanes fly through the air," Gates said. "Is that true?"

"In a way, yes," Sandford said, switching her display to check the life-support system. "A sub's large dive planes give the boat some lift, same as a plane's wings do. And a sub maneuvers more like a plane than a surface ship. Subs and airplanes operate in a three-dimensional environment—up, down, left, right, while surface ships operate in two dimensions."

Sandford switched back to the primary display.

"But this little sub flies more like a helicopter than an airplane," she continued. "We've got individual thrusters to move us forward and backward, side to side, and up and down. Plus, we have additional variable direction thrusters. With these joysticks I can move in any combination of directions. Watch."

Gates saw the speedometer drop to zero as Sandford brought the vessel to a full stop. It hung suspended for a moment, then pivoted three hundred and sixty degrees. The DSV slipped sideways to starboard while descending at a forty-five-degree angle, stopped, rose vertically, stopped again, then moved laterally to port.

"See what I mean?" Sandford said.

Gates nodded. "You maneuvered this thing like it was a flying saucer."

Sandford shrugged. "Yeah, if you believe in that stuff." After a moment, she cocked an eye at Gates. "Do you?"

"Do I what?" Gates said.

"Believe in that stuff—flying saucers, I mean?" she said. "Captain Gunnar said you ran a special team that investigates UFOs and such."

Gates sighed heavily. He rarely spoke to people about the DSF–Papa. Not that doing so was forbidden, but because most people would ridicule the idea.

"Mysterious things happen at sea, Sarah," he finally said. "Sometimes they endanger safety at sea. When they do, it's our job to find out what's causing those mysterious things to happen and, if it's possible, stop them from happening. That's all."

"You mean the Bermuda Triangle?" Sandford asked. "You mean that's real?"

Another sigh from Gates.

"Let me explain it this way, Sarah," he said. "Have you ever heard of the Kraken?"

Sandford's lips pursed in thought, then she shook her head.

"For hundreds of years, mariners told tales of a giant multi-tentacled creature that attacked their ships, and grabbed sailors right off the deck and rigging. Jules Verne had Captain Nemo's sub, the Nautilus, attacked by a Kraken in *Twenty Thousand Leagues Beneath the Sea*."

"Oh, I saw that movie," Sandford said. "The giant octopus, right?"

"A giant squid," Gates corrected. "Squids are much more aggressive than octopi. Anyway, for centuries, science considered Krakens simple sailor stories—sea myths and nothing more. But when bodies of giant squids washed up on beaches—creatures a dozen feet long or more—researchers started wondering just how big a squid could get. Several years ago, scientists sent a remote vehicle into one of the deepest parts of the ocean and guess what they photographed?"

"One of these Krakens?"

"Well, a monster squid. Researchers estimate their size can range from thirty to sixty feet long and weigh up to a ton," Gates said.

"That's a lot of calamari," Sandford said

"Yes, and more than large enough to attack a vessel the size of ancient sailing ships."

Sandford glanced out at the black water surrounding them.

"Could these things be around here?"

Gates shook his head.

"Too shallow," he said. "They prefer deep water and only come up to feed. My point is, Sarah, strange stuff happens at sea, but most often they have a reasonable, natural, or scientific reason for happening. Our mission is to discover what that reasonable or scientific reason is."

"So that's why you have Dr. Baby Face and the rest of you over-educated swabbies, right?"

Gates chuckled. "Dr. Baby Face," he mused. "I've got to remember that."

"Oh, he's cute," Sandford said, "but terribly young. I prefer my men to have some maturity."

She gave Gates a sidelong glance. He blushed and felt a nervous lump form in his throat. Before he could respond, Sandford turned to the sonar display.

"What's that?" she said, pointing to the side-scan sonar image.

Gates studied the image, a computerized rendering of the sea bed made up of shades of black and brown, with hints of yellow. A large object sat upright on the sea bed. Gates made out the curve of a bow. A flat deck house ran the length of the object, with a single protrusion from the center. Behind the deck house, the stern sloped off and disappeared into the ocean mud.

"It's a boat," he said, recognizing the shape. He felt sick and uneasy. "We better check it out."

Sandford picked up the microphone.

"Franklin, Chip-1. Side-scan has picked up a large object to our port side," she said. "Commander Gates wants to investigate. We're descending to the sea floor."

As the DSV approached the ocean bottom, Sandford turned on the external lights, casting the dark floor into brilliant daylight. Gates watched with wonder the abundant sea life. Brightly colored sea stars, snow and hermit crabs, sea snails, and worms scuttled across the frigid mud, while speckled Arctic cod, striped eel fish, snail-fishes, sculpin with wing-like fins, and various salmon darted in and out of the halo of light.

The wonderment faded as the sunken object came into view. The DSV's lights climbed up the burnt-orange hull. R/V FRANKLIN, stenciled in black, appeared on the vessel's bow. Sandford positioned the DSV to the starboard of the vessel. Midships was the small, enclosed coxswain station, one view-port cracked by a hole. Beyond the broken glass, Gates saw the face of the coxswain, one dead eye opened and staring back at him like the dull, lifeless eye of a landed fish.

"Is that what I think it is?' Sandford choked.

"The Franklin's missing lifeboat," Gates said. "And inside, her missing crew."

Chapter 15

T he Franklin carried a single, fully enclosed, self-righting lifeboat mounted in a free-fall launch railing on the starboard side. It was among best lifeboat escape systems on the market. For the crew of the Franklin, it had become a death trap.

Sarah Sandford stared at the wreckage, the usual humor that graced her face gone, replaced with a look of horror.

"Are those bullet holes?" Her voice was a mere croak

Machine gun bullets ruptured the boat's fiberglass hull. Not light automatic fire either, Gates figured. Something with a large caliber had done that damage. Those on board not killed outright by the heavy weapons fire drowned as the lifeboat settled to the bottom of the Chukchi Sea. Various denizens of the deep scurried in and out of the torn hull, no doubt feeding on the bodies inside.

"Yes," Gates said, his own voice tight. "I need this position plotted and recorded. We'll need to send another ship out to retrieve the boat and the—"

He didn't need to finish the sentence.

"It's already recorded by our inertial guidance system," Sandford said. She looked at the navigation system and read out the latitude and longitude.

"Can we videotape this?" Gates asked.

Sandford reached up to an overhead control panel and pressed a button.

"Recording," she said.

"I want everything," Gates said. "Stem to stern, topside, port, and starboard. Everything."

"Aye," Sandford replied.

"Good." Gates picked up Gertrude's microphone and hailed the Franklin. Salcedo answered, and Gates asked for Leland Strange. "We found the missing lifeboat, Leland. It's been sunk by what appears to be machine-gun fire. We can see one body. We have to assume the rest of Franklin's crew is inside."

"My god," Strange said. "Who the hell . . ."

"I need you to get on the sat phone and call Admiral Rickert. Tell him about the lifeboat and give him this position." Gates read off the lat and long. "He needs to get a recovery mission started. And tell him what Sarah and I are doing. If he bitches—and he will—tell him I assume full responsibility. You got that?"

"Yes, sir," Strange said.

"We're recording video of the damage now," Gates continued. "I'll get that to him as soon as we get back."

He thought, but didn't say, if we get back.

"Roger that, sir," Leland said.

When they finished videotaping the wreck, Sandford resumed their original course to the Vilanovsky. Her demeanor had changed. She no longer lectured Gates or teased him. A tight grimace replaced the seductive smile. Her eyes glistened with tears she refused to cry. When she did talk, it was simply to acknowledge Gates' questions with a quiet, "Yes, sir" or "No, sir."

Gates understood the change. He had seen it before. Faced with the sudden reality of the situation, she was falling back on her military training, focusing on her duties, and trying not to think too much beyond those duties. For the next hour, they traveled in silence.

"There it is," Sandford said, pointing to the forward-looking sonar screen. The Vilanovsky's large concrete caisson appeared on the display. With each minute of approach, it loomed larger, until it filled the screen. Sandford touched a button, and the side-scan image disappeared, allowing the caisson image to dominated the entire screen.

"What's that?" Gates asked, pointing to a darker area on one side of the caisson.

"It looks like . . ." Sandford studied the image before continuing. "Like an opening."

"Into the caisson?"

"It sure looks it, commander." Sandford reached for the twin joysticks. "I'll get us closer."

"No, no," Gates said. "Let's sit here and watch for a while. I don't want to stumble blindly into anything."

"Aye," Sandford said. "I'll settle her onto the floor."

They watched. At this distanced and depth, they could not see much through the viewing bubble. Yet a strange glow leaked out of the opening.

"What's that light?" Sandford asked.

"Work lights," Gates said. "They have several DSVs and deep-diving suits. My guess is they're working on whatever they have under the platform."

"They have something *under* the Vilanovsky?"

"When we were aboard, Dr. Baby Face saw notes on a lab whiteboard. It mentioned energy emissions coming from an object beneath the platform. He also overheard a couple workers talking about what they called 'that thing below.'"

Sandford chuckled. Gates looked her, puzzled.

"You call him Dr. Baby Face," she said.

Gates grinned. "I told you I'd remember that name."

They waited ten more minutes and then, spotting nothing unusual, Gates patted Sandford's shoulder.

"All right," he said, "let's go."

Sandford took the controls, and Chip lifted off the ocean floor, its horizontal thrusters creating small tornadoes of sea mud. She eased the sub forward, but it was sluggish to the command. She applied more power, but the DSV acted as if it were dragging an anchor.

"What the hell?" she muttered.

"What is it, Sarah?" Gates asked.

"I . . . I think we're stuck on something. Maybe a cable?"

Sandford's fingers stabbed at the video controls. The displayed screen switched to video feeds from cameras forward and aft, and port and starboard. This deep, three segments of the screen were dark. But the fourth, from the aft-mounted camera showed two light sources and, behind those, a metallic glint. Sandford switched on the stern light, revealing a man in a deep-diving suit, the articulated torso and extremities resembling a modern rendition of the venerable Robbie the Robot, including the pincer-like hands. The diver held Chip clenched in those pincers.

"Oh, my god, look!"

Sandford pointed through the window at two small two-man DSVs rising from the uneven ocean floor. They sped toward Chip with their mechanical arms extended, hands snapping menacingly.

"Get us out of here," Gates said.

"No fucking kidding," Sandford muttered.

Her fingers danced over the video-screen controls, switching displays. The propulsion screen appeared, and

Sandford activated the backup batteries she said gave the mini-sub an extra "oomf." Grabbing the joysticks, she swung Chip 180 degrees. The diver, still hanging onto the sub stern, spun with the DSV, and slammed into one of the Vilanovsky's approaching subs. Gates watched the screen as the diver, his helmet glass shattered, sank out of view. Chip, its weight lightened, sprang upward and forward, away from the pursuing Russians.

"Nicely done," Gates said, craning to spot the Russians.

"Sit down and shut up," Sandford said, switching the display screen back to the four camera views. Gates did as he was told, and Sandford added softly, "sir."

High-powered lamps on the Russian DSVs sliced through the darkness of the sea. A third DSV rose from behind a sea mount to starboard, its wavering beams stabbing through the dark. The lights fell on Chip, enveloping the small submersible in blinding light that grew more intense as the Russian subs raced to intercept it.

The smaller Russian DSVs were faster than Chip. Despite the extra power from Chip's batteries, the Russians closed. One extended its mechanical arm its full length and tried to grab Chip's landing skids. Sandford side-slipped Chip to port and the Russian's claw closed on sea water alone. A second Russian came at them from the port side, its mechanical hand stretched out, ready to grab onto Chip. Sarah side-slipped again, this time to starboard, and the hand bit down on nothing.

The third Russian sub came hurdling at them from starboard, its grasper arm retracted and with such speed Sandford knew he intended to ram them. Sandford whipped Chip around to the right and sent it scuttling to port. The Russian careened off Chip's starboard hull with an ear-splitting clang, then limped off into the dark.

The remaining two Russians came at Chip from both sides, their motorized arms retracted. Sandford understood they were no longer trying to capture the DSV but sink it. She realized something else. She smiled and murmured, "They're thinking in two dimensions."

Both Russians lurched forward, their thrusters churning the sea. As they raced toward Chip, the little sub slowed and stopped. Before Gates could question why, a great weight pushed him deeper into his chair as Chip shot upward, out of the grasp of the Russians. The two Russian DSVs collided head on with a crunch heard inside Chip. In one camera view, Gates and Sarah watched a crack form on the Plexiglas window of a Russian sub. The Russian hung suspended for a moment, then settled toward the bottom. Its two companion DSVs grabbed it on both sides and tried lifting it to the surface.

It was too late. The cracks stretched across the window until it burst inward, flooding the crew compartment. The extra weight tore the DSV from its companions' mechanical hands and carried it to the sea floor.

Sandford drove Chip at its fastest speed toward the international maritime boundary. When the inertial guidance system showed they were in American waters, she slowed, surfaced Chip, and set a course for the Franklin.

She sat back in her chair and looked at Gates. Her lips where trembling, and her hands shook. Neither spoke. Gates reached for her, to offer a comforting touch, but his own hand trembled, and he drew it back.

Half an hour later, they were back aboard the research ship.

Chapter 16

I just got off the sat phone with Admiral Rickert."
Gates stood at the front of the conference room. His team
was sitting around the long table, as was Captain Gunnar
and his chief mate, Gerry Salcedo. Sarah Sandford was ab-
sent. He didn't need to ask why.

"Considering what we found—the Franklin's missing
crew in the sunken lifeboat—and the ambush Sarah and I
experienced, he has ordered us to stand down from any
more—the word he used was 'activities'—aimed at the Vilanovsky," Gates said, his voice somber. He glanced around
the table and cleared his throat.

"I should not have authorized that mission," he continued. "Military service is inherently dangerous. We recognize what could happen to us. But Sarah didn't sign up for
what we do. By using her to spy on the Vilanovsky, I put
her in danger and, by extension, the civilian mariners on this
ship." He turned to Gunnar. "For that, Captain Gunnar, I ac-
cept full responsibility and offer my deepest apologies."

Silence lingered until Gunnar scooted back his chair
with a loud screech and stood.

"Hogwash!" he said. "That's not the strongest word I
was thinking of using, but it'll do." He thumped himself on
the chest. "I suggested using the DSV. I authorized its use.
If anything, I'm as guilty as you. And I don't give a fig what
Washington thinks. The captain of this ship was a friend of
mine, and he's sitting at the bottom of the ocean, dead. I'm

glad you and Sarah went out. I'm glad you found the lifeboat and their bodies. And I'm glad we now know those bastards on that oil rig are to blame. So, don't go apologizing to me, and don't hog all the responsibility. I deserve some of that, too, and I will tell that to Rickert, by god!"

Gunnar turned and saw the startled faces surrounding him. He sat and, this time, quietly pulled his chair forward. "Well, I had to say that."

"Thank you, captain," Gates said, a small smile turning up the ends of his mouth. "But you won't need to call Admiral Rickert. He wants to see how this shakes out, and whether there is any diplomatic fallout. I don't think there will be, myself. The Russians would have a hard time explaining that machine-gunned lifeboat."

Gates pulled out a chair and sat at the table.

"The admiral told me something else," he said. "He's been butting heads with the Navy over this mission. The Navy owns the Franklin, but it's not a commissioned vessel, and it was being operated by an oceanographic institute with a nonmilitary civilian crew, which puts it under Coast Guard jurisdiction. He even pointed out that the Coast Guard is the senior naval service."

Whoops and cheers erupted from the Coasties. As the Coast Guard was formed in 1790 as the Revenue Cutter Service, eight years before the U.S. Navy's founding in 1798, it is often called the First Fleet, America's first naval force. The Navy, however, claims lineage to the Continental Navy of the American Revolution. Yet, Congress dissolved that small naval flotilla soon after the end of the war, leaving the newly independent country with no naval force until the Cutter Service emerged five years later.

"I bet that made heads explode at the old Navy Yard," said Senior Chief Hopper. He emphasized his point by spitting tobacco juice into a soda can.

"The admiral agreed to a compromise," Gates continued. "He said the Navy is sending an officer out here to secure Navy property."

"Shit, the Navy couldn't keep track of the Franklin before," Senior Chief Hopper said. "What makes them believe one zero can now?" After a moment, Hopper realized he'd used a less-than-respectable slang word for an officer, and mumbled, "Sorry, sirs."

Gates ignored Hopper and continued. "He'll arrive tomorrow by helo. So, until then, turn-to and stand by to stand by."

☼

Gates rapped on Sarah Sandford's cabin door. She cracked the door, saw who it was, then opened it and stood back as Gates entered. Gone was the thick, warming clothing she wore on the DSV. A snug sweat shirt and matching pants showed the curves of her athletic figure. The shirt bore the name and silhouette of a research ship Gates didn't know. Her eyes were red and dried tears streaked both cheeks. She held a cup from the galley in one hand, and Gates could smell wine on her breath.

"Merlot?" she asked. When Gates glanced curiously at two wine bottles on the cabin's small writing desk, she added, "This isn't a dry ship, commander. You go into any cabin, and you'll find someone's personal stash. The Franklin is strictly BYOB."

"Sure," Gates said, wondering if his own team had made similar discoveries. "Why not? We deserve it."

Sandford found another cup and filled it. Gates picked it up, clicked cups with her, and drank.

"So how can I help you, commander?" Sandford asked.

"I wanted to tell you two things," Gates said. "First, I apologize for putting you in danger today. It was irresponsible of me. And, two, I wanted to thank you for getting us out of trouble."

Sandford looked at him a moment, then snorted. "Sit down."

She directed Gates to the desk chair. She sat cross-legged on the bunk.

"This ain't my first rodeo, commander," she said. "Navy DSV pilots get involved in all kinds of secret squirrel operations. Today was just another day at the office."

She gently wiped an eye. When she saw the look on Gates face, she said, "Yes, I've been crying, but not because I was scared. I've been scared before. So, have you. It goes with the business. I cried because . . ."

She took a sip of wine, uncrossed her long legs, and sat with her elbows on her knees, looking at Gates.

"I told you I knew the two DSV pilots who were on this ship, right?" Gates nodded. "What I didn't tell you is I was involved with one of them, Johnny Holcomb. Not that we were lovers—well, not for a long time. We decided we were better as friends than lovers. And Johnny was my best friend, my big brother in a way."

Sandford sighed. Her lips trembled, and tears glistened in her eyes.

"God, I'm going to miss you, Johnny," she whispered. She took another drink before turning away to wipe her tears.

Gates placed his wine on the nightstand and stood. He wanted to comfort her, to hold her in his arms and be the big brother she was now missing. Instead, he cleared his throat and murmured, "I'm sorry for your loss, Sarah."

When she said nothing in reply, Gates turned toward the door. His hand was on the knob when she said, "You remind me of Johnny. Almost from the minute we met, out there on the helo pad, you reminded me of Johnny."

He turned, and she was facing him with a coy smile.

"Tall, dark, and handsome," she said, "with an over-active sense of responsibility."

"And all this time I thought you didn't like me," Gates said.

Sandford knitted her brow, and the smile evaporated. "What made you think that?"

Gates shrugged. "Some things you said gave me the impression you didn't hold me in high regard. You know, the teasing and stuff."

Sandford rolled her eyes, and she muttered, "Oh, for god's sake."

She placed her cup on the night stand, walked up to Gates, and wagged her finger in his face.

"That's another thing about you that reminds me of Johnny," she said. "You're a little slow on the uptake."

She kissed him lightly on the mouth.

"Can't you tell when a woman is flirting with you, commander?"

Gates found his arms wrapped around Sandford, his tongue tasting the wine on her lips, the firmness of her breasts pushing into his foul weather coat, her groin pressing into his. When they broke apart, he said, "My first name is Doug. But you knew that, didn't you?"

"Yes, commander," she said.

"You can call me that now."

"Yes, commander," she said. "But only in private."

"We're in private now."

"There's something you should know . . . Doug," she said. "I lied to you this morning when we were getting into Chip."

Gates looked at her, puzzled. "About what?"

She smiled and drew herself into him.

"I actually am a cuddler," she said.

Chapter 17

Sergey Novikov, the Vilanovsky's operations director, stopped at the conference room door and listened. Something had happened in the morning, something serious. Some men were killed in a terrible undersea accident was all he knew. Was all he was *told*, he thought, which miffed him. He *was* director of operations, after all, and he should be informed of these things. Ever since, Konstantin and Praskovya had been locked in the meeting room. There was no yelling, only muffled urgent voices, the words unrecognizable. Two workers walked by, slowing and eying Novikov as he hovered at the door, listening. He shooed them away. Then, looking at the printed equipment failure reports in his hand, he decided they could wait and hurried down the passageway to his office.

Inside the conference room, Konstantin poured his fourth or fifth sweet coffee of the morning. He couldn't remember. Praskovya sat across the table from him smoking what must have been his twelfth cigarette of the day. Tobacco smoke hung in the air like a London fog.

"Once more, let us go through it again," Konstantin said. Praskovya's eyes rolled. "Now, Petya."

"Our underwater acoustic sensors picked up their DSV's scanning sonar and alerted us to their approach," Praskovya said. "We heard them far off, so we laid a trap."

"And I warned you about your damn fancy tricks, Petya," Konstantin said, interrupting.

"Yes. Yes, you did, Aleks," Praskovya sighed.

"Go on," Konstantin urged.

"My men took three of our small submergence vehicles and a deep-diving suit and lay in wait for them. When the Americans approached the Vilanovsky, we attempted to apprehend them."

"Then what?"

"We failed," Praskovya said, exhaling another cloud of smoke.

"Why?"

Praskovya shrugged. "My men who were there said the American DSV pilot drove it like a jet fighter or a helicopter. They'd never seen such maneuvers."

Praskovya took another deep drag and let the smoke curl from his mouth.

"You were correct, Aleks, my friend," he said, the gray smoke swirling around him. "I should have kept that little American submarine instead of playing games as I did. There is more to it than I saw."

"You were able to capture it once," Konstantin said, "why not again?"

The security chief heaved his shoulders. "A more talented DSV pilot," he said, then muttered, "I wouldn't mind meeting him some day."

"And the losses?"

"Two men in a deep submergence vehicle, another in the diving suit," Praskovya said. "And, of course, the vehicle and the suit."

"Of course," said Konstantin. "And the cover story?"

"For our people here on the Vilanovsky, just that there was an accident while working on that thing below." Praskovya snubbed out his cigarette and prepared another. "For everyone else, we had a diving accident while replacing the drill head. The families of the men have already been notified. They will be handsomely compensated."

"And the Americans?" Konstantin said. "What did they see?"

"Hard to say." Praskovya frowned. "Perhaps they found the remains of the lifeboat. If so, they will know what happened to the Franklin's crew, but not who did it. They may suspect, but they cannot prove it." After a moment, he added, "They may have seen the portal into the caisson."

"What?"

"They seemed to be observing it when our men tried to apprehend them," Praskovya said.

"If they saw the portal, they will realize this is not a drilling operation," Konstantin said. "No drilling platform has such a portal."

"True," Praskovya said. He stared at the ash on his cigarette, feeling unusually sanguine about the whole matter. "Truer words, my friend, have never been spoken."

"Now what?"

Praskovya inched an eyebrow up and looked at his friend. "And now . . . what?"

"You understand what I mean," scolded Konstantin. "We cannot afford to have the Americans know what we are doing here."

"What could they know other than this is a very strange oil drilling platform? What can they deduce from that?"

"Did they see *inside* the portal?"

Praskovya shook his head. "They were too far away," he said. "My people attacked them before they got too close."

"Good. Good." Konstantin paced the floor, hands clasped behind his back. He stopped and turned. "But we cannot be *certain*. Perhaps they had sensors that read energy emissions."

"I found nothing on board when we had the vessel in our custody capable of reading energy emissions," he said. "I made certain of that."

"But you cannot be certain," Konstantin blurted. "Perhaps they installed something new. It might not have been the same DSV."

Konstantin was becoming shrill, and Praskovya was enjoying it. He continued his bored countenance.

"There was only one little submarine on the research ship," he said. "It was the same one."

Konstantin continued pacing, shaking his head as he walked. "The Americans or anyone else must not discover what we have here. There may be many more than the one that sits beneath us. With the ice cap diminishing more each summer, we may find many more, many more. If we can learn to harness their power, it will give Russia dominance over the Americans and the Chinese."

"This project is very important," Praskovya agreed.

Praskovya lit his Belomorkanal and waited. The moment was getting close. He had worked with Konstantin for many years, both when Aleks was with the KGB and he was with Spetsnaz, and later, when the oligarchs became the masters of Russia. Aleks was always slow to come to action. But once committed, Aleks would fully back his actions.

"Petya?" Konstantin had stopped pacing. He faced Praskovya, his jaw set and rigid.

"Yes, Aleks?" *This is it.*

"We can no longer chance American spying or interference," Konstantin said. "We must dispose of that ship and everyone on it."

Praskovya sat up and crushed his cigarette into the ash-
tray.

"You want me to sink the Franklin?"

"And everyone and everything on board her."

"You remember there is American military on board
the Franklin now?" Praskovya said.

Konstantin nodded. "They didn't look particularly dangerous. The young African officer looked more a school
boy than a soldier. Can you do it, Petya?"

Praskovya nodded, his lips puckering in thought.

"If there is a firefight, we might lose a man or two, but
we can do it," he said.

"And the explosives? Can you make sure they work this
time?"

"We can manufacture new detonators—mechanical
detonators," Praskovya said. "There should be no problem
this time."

"Fine, Petya. When can you make this so?"

"We will need time to make the detonators and develop
an assault plan," Praskovya said. "Not tonight, but tomorrow night, I think."

"Good, do it then," Konstantin said. He turned toward
the door to leave, but Praskovya called out to him.

"Aleks?"

"Yes, Petya?"

"This thing below," Praskovya said. "Is it really worth
chancing World War III?"

Konstantin paused a moment, then nodded. "Yes,
Petya. Yes, it is."

Chapter 18

The Navy CH-53 Sea Stallion hovered low over the Franklin's helo pad. A thick length of fast rope dropped, and a man in desert BDUs slithered to the deck. The crew chief released the rope and let it fall to the deck and lowered an overstuffed olive-drab parachute bag on a cable connected to a power hoist. The new arrival waited for the bag to settle on the pad, disconnected it from the cable, and gave the crew chief a thumbs-up. After the Sea Stallion roared off, the man removed his small, Kevlar helmet and replaced it with a stiff, eight-cornered Marine Corps-style fatigue cap. He carried a sidearm in a thigh-rigged holster.

Gates turned to Leland Strange. "The Navy has landed," he said.

The new arrival hefted the parachute bag onto his left shoulder, approached Gates, and saluted. He was tall, broad shouldered, and husky. He had youthful good looks, his fair-skinned face squared-chinned and wide, and freckled and reddened by the sun.

"Lieutenant Carl McCabe, Navy SEALs," he said with a slight drawl.

Gates returned the salute. He introduced himself, then Leland. "They sent a Navy SEAL to secure the Franklin?" Gates asked.

The SEAL studied the younger officer as if he were a laboratory specimen. "One ship, one Navy SEAL, sir."

"I thought the saying was one riot, one Texas Ranger," Gates said.

"I am from Texas, commander," McCabe said, without smiling.

"Ah-huh," Gates muttered. "Lieutenant, what is your mission here?"

McCabe looked at Gates with unflinching blue eyes. "That's on a need-to-know basis, sir."

"Listen, lieutenant," Gates said, returning the SEAL's taciturn stare. "The Franklin may be owned by the Navy, but it's not a commissioned Navy ship. It was being operated by a civilian oceanographic school and manned by a civilian crew with no relationship to the Navy. That means it falls under the U.S. Coast Guard's jurisdiction. That makes me the ranking military officer aboard the Franklin. Is that understood?"

McCabe's jaw muscles tensed and flexed, but his stare didn't waiver. "Understood, sir."

"Fine," Gates said. Without releasing his own stare, he said to Leland, "Lieutenant Strange, please find Lieutenant McCabe a berth . . . in the crew's quarters, if you please."

"Aye, aye, sir," Strange said. He nodded once toward the ladder, turned smartly, and walked away. He didn't bother to look to see if the SEAL followed him.

McCabe glanced at Strange, then back to Gates. Gates' face remained frozen.

"Dismissed, lieutenant," Gates said.

McCabe shook his head, turned, and followed Strange toward the ladder.

After they were out of hearing distance, Gates thumbed the push-to-talk button on his radio. "Hopper, Gates."

"Hopper, sir," came the senior chief's reply.

"Our Navy guest is aboard now," Gates said. "I want him under constant observation. From a distance, of course. Let me know the minute he starts snooping around that secret cubbyhole."

"Aye, sir."

"And, senior chief?"

"Yes, sir?"

"I want our people armed with side arms at all times now, no matter what they're doing."

There was a long pause before the radio squelched and Hopper asked, "Are we going to war with the Navy, sir?"

"Just do it. Gates out."

The radio squelched twice in his ear, Hopper's nonverbal acknowledgment.

Gates took a deep breath, puffed up his cheeks, and exhaled. He rolled his neck, trying to loosen the knots, and murmured his response to Hopper's question.

"I hope not, senior," he said. "I certainly hope not."

"Gates, Hopper," the commander's radio squealed

"Gates, go," he answered.

"Sir, our Navy guest must be in a hurry," Hopper said. "He wasted no time locating that hidden compartment."

"He's there now?"

"Yes, sir. Inside with the hatch closed."

"Good," Gates said. "Muster the team around the corner from the compartment—quietly. I'll be right down."

Gates took the ladders going below decks at a run, using his hands to slide down the railings. Once on the third deck, he slowed and quieted his approach. He found the rest of DSF–Papa positioned as ordered, carrying sidearms and wearing ballistic vests. Gates addressed them in a whisper.

"Our Navy guest, Lieutenant McCabe, reported aboard this morning," he said. "I'm not certain he is who he says he is. In light of what happened to the Franklin's crew, I'm not taking any chances. I want to know what he's doing in that compartment and why. He's not the friendly type, nor is he very communicative. I'm afraid if we knock politely, he's likely to start shooting or even blow himself up. I hope I'm wrong, but, as I said, I'm not taking chances. Understood?"

The team answered in head nods.

"Okay, we do this like any dynamic entry," he continued. "Lieutenant Strange, I want you to guard the far end of the passageway. Block him if he tries to run. Shoot him if you have to. Chief Stalk, you block this end. Frank, you've got the door. You have your aid bag?"

Chee pivoted to display the medical bag strapped to his back, then tapped the gunshot kit secured to his thigh.

"Good. Senior Chief, you and Jess are with me in the stick. First me, then you, then Jess."

"Aye, sir," Hopper said.

Gates looked everyone over and made sure they were only armed with sidearms.

"We're doing this with handguns only," he said. "I don't want a bunch of rounds from auto fire ricocheting off the bulkheads and hitting us. All right, let's move out."

They moved into position, keeping the rattle of their gear to a minimum, each step landing on the full sole of their boots to muffle their steps. Strange moved ahead of them, taking cover around the far corner of the passageway. Chee took position on the left side of the door. Gates, Hopper, and Brown crouched to the right of it.

Gates turned and patted Hopper's knee, making sure he was paying attention. Hopper patted Brown's knee. Gates pointed to himself, then crooked his right index finger, a form of sign language used by tactical teams.

I'll go the left.

He pointed to Hopper and crooked the index finger of his left hand.

You go right.

To Brown, he made a straight up and down motion with his hand.

You're in the middle.

Gates looked at Chee, then the other two, and held up three fingers.

On three.

Chee moved to the door, his right hand finding the concealed door latch, and nodded. Gates held up his left fist and pumped it. The first finger extended. Another pump, and the second finger extended. Three fingers went up and Chee hauled on the camouflaged door, swinging it open. Gates slipped through, dodging to the left of the small compartment, his weapon extended and aimed. Hopper followed, crouching to the right, his Glock aimed and ready. Brown remained outside the door, between Gates and the senior chief, his pistol pointing straight into the compartment, directly at Lieutenant McCabe.

Gates had to give it to McCabe. The SEAL was fast. He drew and readied his own pistol, a Glock 19, the instant the door swung open. He didn't even move from his seat.

"Don't think about it, lieutenant," Gates said.

As Gates spoke, Chee appeared behind Brown, pistol ready. McCabe looked at the four Glocks aimed at him, half puckered his mouth, nodded, and holstered his weapon.

Gates turned to his people and said, "Stand down." They relaxed and holstered their weapons.

"How'd you all find out about this?" McCabe asked.

"We're the Coast Guard," Gates said. "Finding hidden compartments aboard ships is what we do for a living."

"When did you find it?

"The first day on board."

McCabe leaned back and sighed. "They were afraid of that. That's why they sent me. Did you examine at the equipment?"

Gates nodded. "Everything you need for a spy ship. Miniaturized and automated to collect data and burst transmit it."

The SEAL nodded. "Only it's not burst transmitting," he said. "Not for days, even before the Franklin and its crew went missing." He tapped a large box beneath the starboard counter. "This is an uninterruptible power supply. Even when the ship's power is off, it should have continued recording and sending. But *nada*."

"They send a SEAL instead of an electronics technician?" Gates sounded doubtful.

"I have an engineering degree in electronics, commander," McCabe said.

"That's nice," Gates said. "Chief Stalk!"

Stalk appeared at the doorway. McCabe glanced at her, then Gates, not understanding.

"Chief Stalk here has two engineering degrees in electronics," Gates said. "Maybe she can help you trouble shoot."

McCabe looked at Stalk, his brow knitted, and considered the offer. Finally, he shook his head.

"Sorry, commander," he said, "No disrespect, but this equipment is highly classified."

"Chief Stalk also has a top-secret clearance," Gates said. "Same as all of us. And she's worked on similar technology."

The SEAL officer sat back, looked at Gates and the others.

"What kind of Coast Guard unit are you all, anyway?" he said.

"That, lieutenant, is on a need-to-know basis."

Gates' voice was serious, but there was a glint in his eye. McCabe saw it.

"Fair enough," he said, smiling. "In that case, I welcome Chief Stalk's help."

Chapter 19

G ates stepped onto the O-1 deck and looked at the midnight sun hanging low over the horizon. The twilight gloaming fell across the Chukchi Sea, laying a dull sheen on the drift ice thudding into the Franklin's hull. He checked his wristwatch for the fourth time in the past hour, then glanced at the distant light that was the oil platform Vilanovsky.

That evening he had dined with Sarah Sandford in the mess deck, sitting alone in a corner, talking in quiet voices, fully aware of but ignoring the arched eyebrows and pinched grins of the Coasties and CIVMARs. Afterward, they walked to her cabin. She invited him in, but he begged off. There was something unsettling him, something he couldn't describe or explain, something lingering beyond his reach.

Afterward, he *walked the ship*, an old naval term for the captain touring his vessel before a battle. But there was no battle pending; not that he knew of, at least. Still, he paced the upper and lower decks, stopping by the secret compartment where Chief Stalk and Lieutenant McCabe still struggled with the electronics, looking in on Senior Chief Hopper and Jerry Weill, the CIVMAR engineer, still working in main engineering to resurrect the ship's propulsion systems. He climbed one ladder after another up to the O-5 deck and the bridge, where Jess Brown stood watch.

The ship was asleep, except for the watch standers. He leaned against the railing on the O-4 deck, aft and below the DSV control station, and checked the time again. The only sounds were the hollow thuds of ice against metal, the lapping of the water, and the creak of the hull as the Franklin rocked to the sway of the ocean.

"Coffee, commander?"

Gates jumped at the voice. Nikki stood behind him, smiling as usual, a steaming carafe in one hand and a mug in the other.

"Sorry, commander," she said, "I didn't mean to startle you. Captain Gunnar thought you might like coffee."

She filled the mug and handed it to him.

"I thought he was asleep," Gates said, taking the cup.

"He is," Nikki said, still smiling. "I am sorry I startled you."

"Nikki, you have a way of sneaking up on people and then vanishing."

Nikki shrugged. "I am small and make little noise. It is the way of our people. You found what you sought, yes?"

Gates paused with the cup to his lips and raised his eyebrows.

"On your voyage in the small submarine," she added.

"Oh, the lifeboat and the Franklin's crew? Yes."

"I knew you would."

"Why?" Gates asked. "I mean, how did you know?"

"I explained when we first met, commander," Nikki said. "You and I are not unalike. We see more than the others."

"See more what?"

Gates held out his cup for a refill. Nikki took it and poured more coffee.

"Of all things," she said.

"Nikki, what did Captain Gunnar tell you about me?" Gates said, his voice edged with insistence. "Did he say I was psychic or something?"

Nikki's smile disappeared, replaced by puzzlement.

"I do not know that word, commander," she said. "But, no, he never used it about you. Captain Gunnar has told me nothing about you. Please drink your coffee, commander. It is a fine night, and you should be alert."

Gates finished his cup again, and Nikki refilled it.

"What do you mean I should be alert?" he asked.

Nikki looked over Gates' shoulder, her large almond-shaped eyes narrowing, as if focusing on something in the distance. He turned and scanned the ocean out to the horizon.

"Stand your watch, commander," Nikki whispered behind him. "You will see."

Gates turned to ask what she meant by that, but she was gone.

It came only a few minutes later. A dim, shimmering light to the north floating above the horizon. His spine went cold, and dread flooded his soul.

Hands shaking, Gates set his coffee on a nearby bollard, turned, and ran up the stairs to the bridge. Jess Brown was still on watch. He mumbled a "Sir?" as Gates dashed into the wheelhouse, grabbed the gunner's mate's night-vision goggles and binoculars, and scrambled down the stairs to the next deck. Brown followed.

"Sir, what is it?" Brown asked.

Gates ignored the petty officer. He turned the NVGs on and scanned the region to the north, where he spotted the light. The NVGs showed only the Vilanovsky, a small sun in the green and black display, and chunks of sluggish, green-shaded drift ice moving with the current. He lowered the goggles, trading them for the binoculars, but still no flickering light. He lowered those, too, and searched the shadowy sea with his naked eye.

Still nothing.

"Sir?"

Gates looked at Brown, thankful that the dim sunlight hid the frightened look on his own face and shook his head.

"Sorry, Jess," he said. "Thought I saw something out there. Probably only starlight reflecting off the ice. Let me hold on to these just to make sure."

"Yes, sir." Brown turned and took the stairs back to the bridge two at a time.

Gates stood against the railing for several minutes, breathing slow and deep to calm the pounding in his head and chest. *Just what I need,* he thought, *more rumors about my visions.* He remembered what Nikki said. "We see more than the others." Well, in the military that kind of crap can sink your career faster than the iceberg sank the Titanic.

He relaxed and took the coffee mug from the bollard where he had left it and drained the contents. The coffee was cold. He yawned and considered hitting the rack. *Maybe I should make one more tour of the ship.*

He saw it again, this time closer, brighter. He brought up the NVGs; again, nothing but the Vilanovsky and drift ice. Lowering the goggles, the light was there, flickering like a flame. He picked up the binoculars. This time he saw it clearly, an ancient sailing ship, squared-rigged, reaching on a port tack, and glowing as if aflame.

The Flying Dutchman.

He watched as it came about on a starboard tack, heading straight for the Franklin. The dread from minutes ago flooded back in. He stood motionless, unable to lower the binoculars, unable to turn away. His feet felt encrusted in ice, frozen to the deck. His heart pounded from a surge of adrenaline.

The Dutchman tacked again, to port. On the quarter deck of the glowing vessel stood a solitary figure, tall and waving as if to get his attention. The figure turned and pointed behind him, pointing to another light in the distance, pointing toward the Vilanovsky.

The ancient ship continued its port tack, drawing away from the Franklin, growing smaller, dimmer, until it disappeared, even with the glasses. Gates lowered the binoculars, surprised he could move, and turned toward the bridge. With slow, deliberate steps, he climbed the ladder and entered the wheelhouse, set the NVGs and binoculars on a counter, paused to think, then turned to Brown.

"Jess, go below and wake up Lieutenant Strange and the senior chief," he said. "Tell them I want everyone on deck with full battle rattle. The Navy SEAL, too—Lieutenant McCabe. Wake Captain Gunnar and ask him to muster his people on the mess deck. Then bring my kit up here."

"Sir?"

"Do it, Jess," Gates said. "Now."

"Aye, sir."

Brown turned and clambered down the ladders to the sleeping sailors below.

They couldn't have responded faster if he sounded a general quarters klaxon. Leland Strange arrived first, clad in his ODUs, ballistic vest, helmet, sidearm, and M-4 carbine. Gates wondered if the young officer slept in his battle rattle.

Brown came next, loaded with his own kit and Gates'. Lieutenant McCabe followed close behind, adjusting his flak vest as he climbed the stairs. Gates finished fitting his gear on when the last of DSF–Papa reported to the bridge. They formed a circle and waited for his orders.

"This will sound crazy," he said, "but I think we're about to be boarded."

"Boarded?" said McCabe. "By whom, sir?"

"The same people who boarded the Franklin before, killed its crew, and tried to sink the ship." He glanced over his shoulder toward the distant lights of the Vilanovsky.

"The Russians?" McCabe sounded incredulous. "Why?"

"Because of that secret cubbyhole of yours, lieutenant," Gates said. "They tried to sink the Franklin before because they thought the oceanographic equipment on board might have picked up something they didn't want us to know about."

"You mean the object?"

McCabe recognized his mistake the instant he spoke the words. Gates glanced at him with hard, cold eyes, and nodded.

"Yes," he said. "The object. That thing below."

Even in the dim sunlight, Gates spotted the surprise on McCabe's face. *So that's his real mission aboard the Franklin.*

"That's why they degaussed the electronics in the labs," he said. "But they didn't realize the Franklin was a covert spy ship. They didn't know about the sensors in your compartment. But after ambushing Sarah and me in the DSV, they realize we've been snooping around and we're suspicious. And I don't think they can take a chance we might have discovered something about the Vilanovsky and that object."

"Sir, is this supposition," asked Strange, "or did you see some—"

Gates shot the young officer a warning glance.

"I thought I saw something out there," Gates said, taking care to choose his words. "Something not moving with the current or the ice."

McCabe nodded, accepting Gates' reasoning.

"You visited the platform. Do they have the ability to board this ship?"

"We're pretty certain they did it once before," Gates said, nodding. "And their chief of security. What was his name, Leland?"

"Praskovya," Strange said. "Pyotr Praskovya."

"He claims to be a retired navy officer, but he looked too hardened to be an old sea dog. And he has a security force, as Sarah and I discovered."

"I recognize the name," McCabe said. "Ex-Spetsnaz. Known to the intel people for his wild high jinks. No helicopters?"

"One, but a civilian model," Gates said. "Not capable of inserting an armed force."

McCabe nodded again. "In that case, they'd need to come by small boat. They'll come along side and try boarding somewhere close to the bridge. They'll want to take command of that first."

Gates agreed. "That's how we'd do a hostile boarding," he said. "Toss up a line or rope ladder with a grappling hook and climb aboard, hoping to catch the crew asleep."

"Exactly," McCabe said.

"Lieutenant McCabe, I'd like to position you and Petty Officer Brown, our SAW gunner, forward on the O-1 deck. There you both can have a clear field of fire port and starboard if anyone makes it aboard. Also, your radio gear won't talk to ours because of the differing security encryption. Brown can keep you in the link."

McCabe stepped closer to Brown and nodded. "Yes, sir."

"I'll put Senior Chief Hopper midships on the port side main deck, with Petty Officer Chee in the same location on the starboard side. There they can shoot over the gunnel at the boarders while they're still in their boats. Lieutenant Strange, I want you and Chief Stalk aft on the fantail in case they decide not to follow our game plan. I'll locate myself up here so I can keep track of what's going on."

Gates glanced around as heads nodded in approval.

"Everyone monitor the team network, but don't chat it up," he said. "Keep the channel clear except for sitreps."

"Doug? What's going on?"

It was Captain Gunnar, eyes red, hair mussed from sleep.

"Captain, I believe we are about to be boarded," Gates said.

"The Rooskis?"

"Yes. That's why I want your CIVMARs mustered on the mess deck. They'll be safer there."

Gunnar's head shook. "Negative," he said.

"But—"

"But nothing, Doug," Gunnar said. "My people are trained in repelling boarders. Piracy is a constant threat to mariners, as you well know."

"Sir, you have no weapons."

"We have fire hoses," Gunnar said. "You ever been on the wrong end of 400 pounds of water pressure per square inch?"

Gates recalled watching demonstrations of anti-piracy tactics, including using fire hoses and water cannon to defeat boarders. Both were effective.

"Very well, sir," Gates said. "Have your people man fire hoses port and starboard, if you please." He paused, thinking of Sarah. "Perhaps the women can stay in the mess deck?"

"I said *all* my people were trained in repelling pirates, Doug," Gunnar said.

Gates studied Gunnar's face, and his steady blue-gray eyes made it clear there was no point in arguing.

"Very well, captain," he said, nodding. "Make it so."

Chapter 20

T here!"
     All but the Franklin's navigation lights were turned off, leaving the deck below Gates in shadow. He used his night-vision goggles to look down at McCabe and Brown. The SEAL was looking to starboard with NVGs that were at least a generation newer than those issued to the Coasties. McCabe looked up at Gates and pointed. Gates trained his own NVGs in that direction.

They were mere shadows, two dark objects moving against the ice current. They came at low speed, careful not to produce a phosphorescent wake, their motors muffled.

"Two bogeys inbound, starboard side," Gates whispered into this boom mic. "Zero-five-five relative, 300 yards and closing."

A series of clicks answered Gates as members of DSF–Papa acknowledged his report. Gates leaned into the wheelhouse, grabbed the microphone for the loud hailer, and stretched its cord to the starboard search light. Then he waited.

Gates' mouth was dry, his hands wet with sweat. The boats closed on the ship and more details became visible in his NVGs. Rigid-hull inflatables with center consoles, one man standing at each wheel. Shapeless shadows along the side sponsons were the boarding party, impossible to count at this point. As the lead boat drew near, a shadow in the bow rose. That would be the grappler, thought Gates, armed with the grappling hook and its climbing rope or ladder.

Gates swiveled the searchlight, aiming it at the first boat, and thumbed his PTT. "Standby for the searchlight."

Like Gates and McCabe, each member of DSF–Papa had a set of NVGs. Gates assumed the boarders had similar equipment. NVGs worked by magnifying available light. But, if a powerful light source is introduced, the NVGs shut off to protect the viewer's eyes. If the assault team was wearing night goggles, as Gates suspected, switching on the search light should momentarily blind its members.

Gates gave his own team a minute to remove their NVGs and shelter their eyes to preserve their night vision. He flipped the switch on and stepped away from the light.

"This is the United States Coast Guard," Gates said into the loud hailer mic, his voice booming across the drift ice. "You are in American waters. Heave to and lower your weapons."

The only response was a burst of automatic gunfire that shattered the lamp and showered Gates with shards of broken glass.

Well, that didn't work too well, he thought.

"Jess, give them a warning burst," Gates said into his radio.

The SAW gunner stitched the ocean in front of the lead Russian. The Russians responded with their own automatic fire, rounds pounding the bulkhead below where Brown and McCabe were sheltering.

"So much for diplomacy, skipper," Brown said into his radio.

Gates heard the clatter of a grappling hook hitting the main deck. He watched it snag on the inside of the gunwale's tumblehome and become taut. One of the CIVMARs darted out from the air castle, cut the rope with a knife, and ran back for cover. A second grappling hook flew over the gunwale and took hold. The CIVMAR rushed forward again. A hail of blind fire pounded into the side of the ship, sending the CIVMAR scurrying back to cover.

"Chee, fire a burst over their heads, and have the CIVMARs move forward with their fire hose."

Chee acknowledged Gates' order with an immediate burst. The CIVMARs rushed forward and released the stream of a fire hose onto the assault boat. Russian curses and the sound of bodies splashing overboard filled the night. The fire hose tactic was nonlethal, but in the Arctic temperatures exposure to the hose stream or, worse, immersion in the ocean could cause hypothermia and be as deadly as a gunshot wound.

Gates grunted, gratified, then realized he had lost track of the second Russian boat. He scanned the water off the starboard side of the ship and found nothing. He cursed himself for fixating on the lead boat. *Where was that damned second boat?*

"Boarders on the fantail!"

Leland's voice crackled through Gates' earpiece.

"Boarders on the fantail!"

"Damn it," Gates cursed again, spun, and threw himself down the port side ladder to the main deck. When he reached it, he saw Senior Chief Hopper running through the air castle toward the stern. Two rifle flashes and Hopper fell backwards.

"Man down, port air castle!" Gates yelled into his mic.

Ahead of him, a shadow emerged, a dark form against the faint light. Gates raised his M-4, slung from his harness on a three-point sling. The other man fired twice. Gates saw the flashes but no report.

A round passed his ear with an angry bee-like buzz. The second round slammed into the stock of Gates' rifle, shattering it, and ripping it from his hands. Gates tumbled to the left through an open door just as two more rounds screamed pass.

Gates' right hand was numb. With his left hand, he pulled a thin, cylindrical grenade from a pouch on his armored vest, pulled the pin, and tossed it into the air castle. The stun grenade erupted with thunder and lightning.

Gates jumped to his feet, shook his numb hand once, and pulled his expandable baton from its vest holster. He flicked his wrist, and the metal baton expanded to its full length. He stepped out onto the air castle.

The Russian was on one knee, holding both hands to his ears. Gates dashed toward him, but the Russian recovered. He stood, ripped the NVGs from his eyes, and reached for his weapon. It was too late. Gates swung the baton underhanded and struck the man between the legs. It wasn't a conventional baton strike, but it was the only place Gates knew wasn't protected by body armor.

The Russian folded with a cry of pain. Gates side stepped him and brought the baton down on the nerve-rich area between the man's shoulder and neck. It was a paralyzing blow, and the Russian dropped to one knee again. Gates, catching a glance of the prone senior chief, wasn't finished with the man. He aimed the baton to the man's outer thigh, hitting the nerve bundle that ran close to the surface of the skin. The Russian's leg gave out, and he collapsed to the deck.

More gunfire and yells came from the fantail. Gates turned to follow them but thought better of it. He grabbed the Russian's ballistic vest and, with more strength than he thought he had, lifted him up and over the railing. The son-of-a-bitch could drown or freeze to death as far as he was concerned. Another glance at the senior chief's body assuaged any guilt.

Gates banged the tip of his baton on the deck, retracting it, and returned it to its holder. He pulled his Glock and hurried onto the fantail. The starboard CIVMAR team was brandishing their fire hose over the side at the second assault boat, Frank Chee and Chief Stalk covering them with their M-4s. From his right came an angry grunt. Gates swung around with his pistol extended. In the shadow of the giant A-frame crane he saw Leland Strange restrained from behind by a Russian.

"Hey!" Gates combat-walked forward, his pistol leveled at the Russian, but he couldn't get a clear shot. "Hey!"

Leland jerked forward, lifting the Russian onto his back, then threw himself backward. They fell, landing with a loud crack as the boarder's helmet slammed onto the metal deck. Gates heard the air knocked out of the Russian. Leland leapt to his feet, turning toward his assailant, taking up a fighting stance. The Russian regained his feet, too, and attempted a roundhouse kick that Strange easily deflected. Leland went on the offensive, pummeling the Russian with several short, jabbing punches to the face, followed by a solid kick to the man's ballistic vest. The Russian staggered back but was undaunted. He uttered a curse and drew his fighting knife. Rather than drawing his sidearm, Leland resumed his fighting stance.

A loud crack. A red flare arced through the semi-dark sky. A recall signal.

The intruder cursed again in Russian, and Leland replied in kind. The Russian spit on the deck and dashed across the fantail. In one leap, he flew over the life lines into the sea.

A moment later, the Russians were speeding away in their assault boats, the engines unmuffled, not concerned with making noise or leaving a phosphorescent wake. Gates watched them go, remembered the senior chief, and turned to find the team medic.

"Frank, senior chief's hit. Port air castle!"

"I'm all fucking right, skipper."

Senior Chief Hopper limped along the deck, plucking at something on his chest.

"That damn flash-bang you set off hurt me more than these," he said. He handed Gates two smashed bullets, then rubbed his ears. "Damn ears are still ringing."

Gates examined the bullets. "Looks like nine-millimeter."

"Yeah. Probably a machine pistol with a suppressor," Hopper said. "Maybe an MP5 or an Uzi." He looked down and admired the tightly spaced holes in the cloth cover of his ballistic vest. "Nice grouping, though."

"Come on, senior, let's get that vest off and look at your chest." Chee took Hopper's arm and led him away.

Gates approached Strange and put an arm around the young officer.

"You okay, Leland?"

Strange pushed his glasses higher on his nose.

"Sure, sir."

"Where in hell did you learn to fight like that?"

Leland smiled, his white teeth shining in the dim light.

"It's not easy being a boy genius, sir," he said. "Everyone wants to beat you up. My dad figured that out early and enrolled me in karate classes when I was eight. I hold a third-degree black belt."

He removed his helmet, pulled his balaclava from a cargo pocket, and wiped sweat from his hair and face.

"When I was studying in Russia, I took up Systema," he continued. "It means The System. It's a martial art form used by the Russian military, including their commandos. That guy was surprised I knew it."

"What was it he said to you before he jumped over the side?"

"He called me a motherfucker."

"And you replied?"

Leland smiled again.

"I said, 'Only yours.'"

"Lieutenant," Gates said, chuckling, "you now have a new collateral duty—as the team's defensive tactics instructor."

"Happy to do it, sir."

Jess Brown and the Navy SEAL wended their way through the CIVMARs and their hose in the starboard air castle, Brown carrying his SAW over his shoulder and smoking a cigarette. Gates waved McCabe over.

"Lieutenant, a word if you please." He motioned for the SEAL to follow him toward the A-frame, away from the others.

"I appreciate your help tonight, lieutenant," he started, "but now I want answers."

McCabe's face turned to stone. "Sir?"

"Why are you really here?" Gates said. "It's not only to secure that spy gear below decks. I want to know why."

"Sir, that's on a need-to-know—"

"Fine. Let me put it this way," Gates said. "I *need* to know what your real mission is. I have a lifeboat full of dead Americans sitting on the bottom of Chukchi Sea, and we could have ended up the same way tonight. And it has something to do with that Russian oil platform and the OOPART sitting underneath it."

McCabe's eye twitched at the mention of the acronym, but he shook his head.

"All due respect, commander, but I don't have the authority to tell you."

"Then I suggest you get on your sat phone and call your damn superiors and get the authority to read in me and my people. And you tell them if they don't grant that authority to you, my boss will go public with a story about the Franklin's murdered crew, the attack tonight, and how it's tied into the Russians. That'll raise an international stink, and that will not help your mission, will it?"

"No, sir, it would not."

McCabe's mouth puckered in thought, then he nodded.

"I'll do that, commander," he said, turned, and walked away.

Chapter 21

S arah Sandford proved again she was a cuddler. Gates found her with the port side fire hose team, wrapping a first aid dressing around the arm of a CIVMAR who took a grazing wound from a bullet that missed Gates. She looked up at him and gaped.

"My god, Doug! Are you okay?"

"Yeah, why?"

"Your face is bleeding."

He felt his right cheek. It was sticky with congealing blood from several cuts caused by the shards of shattered searchlight glass.

Later, after Frank Chee had removed the shards and cleaned the wounds, Gates took Sarah to her cabin. They lay on the bed clothed, Sarah curling into his left side. He felt her trembling. *From fear? Or the aftereffects of adrenalin?* Gates wasn't sure. But when he held his free arm up, he saw his own hand tremble, too.

She fell asleep. They lay there with the lights on, with Sarah's gentle breathing in his ear, while Gates stared at the overhead and wondered if there was any power in the threat he had told McCabe.

☼

Power or no power, the threat worked. The next morning, Gates and his people mustered in the Franklin's conference room, along with Captain Gunnar, Gerry Salcedo, and Sarah Sandford. McCabe balked at including the latter three but relented when Gates insisted.

"What does it matter?" McCabe muttered. "No one will believe this, anyway. I barely do."

McCabe stood at the front of the room and held his hand up for silence. As the chatter faded to isolated coughs and chair scrapes, the SEAL cleared his throat.

"First, I need to inform you, you all are sworn to secrecy," he said. "Back home, nondisclosure agreements have been filled out for each of you and, I guarantee you, *you have already signed them.*"

The silence deepened. Wary glances around the table. An uncertain chuckle.

"Good," said McCabe. "Now that we know where we stand, let's get going."

He pulled out a chair, sat, and removed a small, black military notebook from his pocket.

"In the first five months of 1968, four submarines from different countries went missing. In January, the Israelis lost the submarine Dakar, followed by the French sub Minerve. Both disappeared in the Med within two days of each other. The next was the Soviet K-129, lost that March in the Pacific, followed by the loss of our own USS Scorpion in May in the Atlantic. To this day, no one knows what happened to them."

"I thought we found the Scorpion's wreckage," Senior Chief Hopper said. Chief Stalk, sitting next to Hopper, jabbed him with her elbow, and he added, "Sir."

"We did, but the destruction was so complete, no cause for the sinking could be determined. There are theories discussed in public, but they're wrong."

"You make it sound as if you know the cause," said Gates.

"I'm getting ahead of myself, commander," McCabe said. "Let me continue. We *do* know what happened to the K-129. We were tracking her with our Pacific SOSUS array when we detected her leaving her normal patrol box at high speed as if she were chasing something. Then we heard an underwater collision, followed by the sound of the K-129 breaking up as she exceeded her crush depth.

"One of our submarines investigated and located the K-129's wreckage. They found something else—the object that collided with the Russian—*whatever it was*."

"'Whatever it was'?" Captain Gunnar said. "And what does that mean, lieutenant?"

"It means, sir, it wasn't another submarine," McCabe said. "Not in the way we think of them. It was lying next to the Russian. It looked lifeless, except it emitted massive amounts of energy. Someone at a higher pay grade than ours decided to retrieve it.

"Wait a minute," Hopper said. "Wait a minute. Now I remember. The K-129 was the sub the CIA tried to raise. Right? They used that big-ass drilling ship owned by Howard Hughes . . . the Glomar Explorer. Isn't that right, lieutenant?"

"Project Azorian," added Gates.

McCabe nodded.

"That's right," he said, "but they weren't after the K-129. They wanted the object it collided with. But as soon as they got the Glomar on scene in 1974, they started having technical issues—electronics crapping out, leaks in hydraulic lines—"

"Like they're having on the Vilanovsky," Strange said. "They blamed them on gremlins."

"Huh." McCabe paused, digesting the information. "Well, that's interesting."

"Go on, lieutenant," Gates said.

"Yes, sir," McCabe said. "When they finally tried to grab the thing with the Glomar's lifting cradle, it came alive. It gave off an energy pulse that hit the Glomar with the force of an explosion. Tore apart the lifting cradle. Flooded one of the forward holds. Fried electronics. Damn near sank the ship, from what I understand.

"It took days, but they got everything back on line, including installing a smaller lifting cradle they used to retrieve part of the Russian sub. But the real prize took off at high speed and disappeared into the North Pacific."

"Toward the Arctic Ocean?" Gates said.

"Toward the Arctic Ocean," McCabe confirmed.

"Lieutenant, are we talking about USOs?" Gates asked. "Unidentified submerged objects?"

"Yes, sir," McCabe said, nodding. "Underwater UFOs. Though the eggheads we deal with call them Unknown Subsurface Phenomena, or USSPs. We call them Fast Movers."

"We?" Gates asked.

"The Navy doesn't talk about it, but we've been investigating Fast Movers—USOs—since the early 1950s. Have you ever heard of Exercise Mainbrace, commander?"

Gates nodded. "A large-scale NATO naval exercise involving a couple hundred ships. The operation was plagued with unidentified aircraft that came out of the sea, then flew back into the sea. High-speed underwater objects, too. There were journalists on the ships who saw the phenomena and published stories about it."

"And the Navy has been studying the phenomena ever since," McCabe said.

"You mean the Navy has a unit like ours?" asked Leland Strange.

McCabe nodded. "I lead one of its teams."

"Probably better funded than we are," muttered Hopper as he spit tobacco juice into his soda can. "Fucking Navy."

Chief Stalk jabbed him again.

"Sir," Hopper added to be polite.

McCabe ignored the senior chief.

"In the decades since," he said, "there have been dozens of reports from around the world, from every navy, of these Fast Movers. The day before the Scorpion went missing, she reported she was tracking one a Fast Mover."

"And you think the Fast Mover the Scorpion was following destroyed her?" asked Strange.

"We think Fast Movers caused the loss of all four boats," McCabe said, "but not the same one that sank the K-129. There must be more than one. After those four boats were lost, every navy in the world issued standing orders for its submarines to avoid these things—not to engage them, or track them, or anything. Turn and run like hell if they have to."

"With all due respect, lieutenant," said Hopper, ever the skeptic, "but you're saying there are fucking underwater flying saucers running around sinking submarines?"

"I'm not telling you anything about what they are, senior," McCabe said with annoyance, "because we don't *know* what they are. Are they some kind of extraterrestrial craft?" McCabe shrugged. "Are they organic?" He shrugged again. "We just don't know."

"You mean they might be sea monsters?" Sandford asked. She looked at Gates. "Like the Kraken you told me about, Doug."

"That's not as outlandish as you might think," Leland said. "The oceans of the Earth are still a mystery to us. We know more about the surfaces of the moon and Mars than our own oceans. We're discovering new marine life every year. And it's not unknown for certain sea creatures to generate electric pulses."

"You mean like an electric eel?" said Chief Stalk.

"Precisely," Strange said. "Though electric eels aren't eels; they're knife fish. But they are a species of electric fish, which also includes electric catfish and electric rays. And they can change the frequencies of their emissions so they don't interfere with the emissions of other nearby electric fish."

"Which might explain the different emissions the Russians were recording on the Vilanovsky," Gates said.

"Possibly, sir," Leland said. "Electric fish use their discharges to stun prey similar to police using a stun gun on suspects. It is not inconceivable a large electric fish predator—say a giant electric ray—could generate enough of a discharge to disable the electronics on a submarine, rendering it inoperable."

"Like an electromagnetic pulse in the atmosphere can knock out electronics on the ground," Stalk said.

"Exactly," Strange said.

"And with the submarine's control systems knocked out, it'll sink until it reaches its crush depth," added Sarah. Her inner thoughts showed on her face. *The greatest fear of submariners—crush depth. Helplessly, hopelessly waiting while the submarine fell through the ocean's depths until the increasing pressure crushed its hull like an egg shell.*

"Let's not go jumping to conclusions," McCabe said. "The Navy's got laboratories full of eggheads who can't figure this out. As I said, it might be mechanical. It might be a form of life. It might be both."

"Let's cut to the chase, lieutenant," Gates said. "Do your people believe whatever the Vilanovsky is sitting over is a Fast Mover?"

"Yes, sir," McCabe said. "We believe these objects seek refuge under the Arctic ice cap, lying dormant for months, years, even decades. Many of our submarines transiting under the ice cap have reported unusual noises they call 'quackers.' They can't be identified as any known mechanical or animal noise, or ice cracking and breaking. They also report encountering high electromagnetic fields, which sometimes interfered with their electronics."

"Geomagnetic anomalies are well known in the Arctic," Strange said. "In 1879, a research ship out of San Francisco became trapped in ice after becoming lost because their compass was malfunctioning. Ice pushed the ship toward New Siberia Island, where it sank. The survivors made it ashore to Siberia near the Lena River Delta and were rescued, but they came back with stories about strange lights they saw below and above the sea."

A puzzled look came over the young officer's face.

"I just remembered something," he said. "When I was studying in Russia, I heard about a secret German U-boat base discovered near the Lena Delta. The people who discovered it in the 1980s found fuel barrels, German Navy uniforms, money, and spare parts for submarines. I thought the story was apocryphal. But what if the Germans knew about Fast Movers and were trying to capture one?"

McCabe shook his head. "Nazi U-boats couldn't go under the ice cap, lieutenant."

"One could," Gates said. "The Walter U-boat." He turned to Sarah. "The one I told you about."

"But you said they never built an operational Walther," Sandford said.

"Not that we know of," the commander said, shrugging. "But if they had a secret submarine base in Russian territory, who knows?"

"This is very interesting," McCabe said, "but perhaps we should come back to the matter at hand?"

'The lieutenant is correct," Gates said. "So, with the melting ice cap, the Fast Movers are losing their refuge. Somehow, the Russians stumbled on one."

"Yes, sir," McCabe said.

"And now the Russians are trying to recover this Fast Mover," Gates said. "They have their own Project Azorian."

"Yes, sir."

"And the Navy is not happy about that."

"No, sir, we're not," said McCabe. "Nor is the CIA, the Pentagon, or the White House. We can't let the Russians have access to whatever this power source is."

"And just what is the Navy, et al., planning to do about it?" Gates asked, certain he already guessed the answer.

McCabe hesitated. After a moment, he sighed and shrugged.

"We're going to destroy the Vilanovsky and whatever lies beneath it," he said.

Chapter 22

How many?"

Aleksandr Konstantin stood at the conference room window staring at the Vilanovsky's upper work deck and the drift ice beyond. The morning sunlight sparkled off the ice. *A beautiful sight.* Despite such reverie, Konstantin clenched his hands behind his back.

"Three," said Praskovya. "Two drowned, one shot. Most of the rest are recovering from varying degrees of hypothermia."

"And how did it happen?" Konstantin demanded.

Praskovya lit a cigarette, inhaled deeply, blew the smoke out.

"They knew we were coming," he said. "They were prepared. We lost the element of surprise. Surprise is everything in this business."

Konstantin turned and braced his hands on the long table.

"And how did they know, Petya?"

Praskovya shook his head. The movement made the smoke hovering around his head turn in little pirouettes.

"I suspect we have a leak," he said. "My people—those capable of getting out of bed—are checking into it. First thing this morning, they checked this room for listening devices, in case the Americans left one behind when they visited. Nothing. Now they are checking every radio message logged, every radio telephone call made, every Internet message sent and received. We will search every cabin for any kind of clandestine messaging device."

"And if they find nothing?"

"They will, Aleks."

"But what if they don't?" Konstantin repeated. "How do we explain the Americans knew your people were coming?"

Praskovya smoked his cigarette, thinking.

"It is possible," he said. "But only possible."

"What damn it?"

"That this platform is under American satellite surveillance," Praskovya said. "There is a possibility they observed us launching the assault boats and radioed the research ship."

"They can do that in the dark?"

"Aleks, we are in the land of the midnight sun," the security officer said. "It is never really dark here in the summer. Yes, it is possible. At least their silly action cinema makes it appear so."

Konstantin paced the room, rubbing his hands together, shaking his head.

"This is terrible," he said. "If we are under satellite surveillance, who knows how much they know?"

"I said it was a mere possibility, Aleks."

Konstantin stopped and spun around. "It is a possibility we must assume is fact," he said, pounding his fist on the table. "This project is far too important for us not to assume the worst."

He crossed the room to a telephone and dialed a number. "Sergey? Konstantin. I need you in the conference room immediately," he said, then hung up.

The door opened less than a minute later, and Novikov entered, carrying a folder bulging with papers.

"Yes, sir?"

"What is our status?" Konstantin demanded.

"Sir?"

"How soon can we lift the object?"

"But, sir, we are still experiencing equipment problems," Novikov said, holding out the thick folder. "The gremlins . . ."

"I don't want to hear about make-believe creatures," Konstantin said. "I am tired of excuses. When can the object be lifted?"

"Mr. Konstantin," Novikov said, "the lifting cradle is in position, but there is still the obstacle—"

"When can the obstacle be removed?"

"We have removed approximately fifty percent of it," said Novikov, "maybe a little less. It must be done by hand—"

"Why?"

"Sir?"

"Why must it be done manually?" Konstantin asked. "Why not use explosives to remove it?"

"Aleks, Aleks," Praskovya said. He lit another cigarette. "If we use explosives, the blast wave would be confined to the interior of the caisson. It might destroy the object we are trying to retrieve. Not to mention this platform."

Konstantin paced again. He waved Praskovya's cigarette smoke away from his face as he spoke.

"We must speed up our progress," he said. "The Americans could discover what we are doing at any time." He stopped and turned on Novikov. "Sergey, you have forty-eight hours to remove the obstacle. If you cannot do so manually, we will risk explosives." He turned to Praskovya. "That, Petya, is your department. There must be a way of breaking apart the obstacle without creating all this damage you mention. Miners blast holes into mountains. How is this different?"

"Aleks," Praskovya said, "water is non-compressible. The blast wave from an underwater explosion is far greater than one from an explosion in the open air or underground."

"I do not care," Konstantin said. "I do not want excuses. In two days, three at the latest, I want that obstacle removed and the object lifted into the moon pool. Do I make myself clear?"

Before they could answer, a tremor shook the floor of the meeting room.

"What is that?" Konstantin demanded.

"I'm not sure, sir," Novikov said. "Machinery? Perhaps they are using the tractor crane on the drilling deck."

The shaking intensified, rattling the coffee service sitting on the table.

"Look!"

Praskovya pointed out the window where a web of support cables strung across the platform were swaying. The tremor died away and the cables slowed their gyrations. Konstantin pushed a button on a wall-mounted intercom.

"Control room? Konstantin speaking. What was that?"

"Sea quake, Mr. Konstantin," was the reply.

"Sea quake? This is supposed to be a geologically staple region."

"Yes, sir," the distant voice said, "but there are active regions deeper into the Arctic Ocean. Maybe we felt shaking from a distant quake."

"Very well," Konstantin said, snapping off the intercom.

"Sir?" It was Novikov.

"What?" Konstantin snapped.

"Sir, I think there may be another solution . . . to the obstacle question."

"Go on."

Novikov adjusted his glasses and wet his lips.

"We might reposition the lifting cradle and use it to move the obstacle aside."

Konstantin stared at the operations director. "That is possible?"

"It is . . . feasible," Novikov said. "Afterwards, we reposition the cradle over the object again."

"Then why did we not do that before?" Konstantin demanded.

"I said it is feasible, sir. That does not mean it is the correct way to remove the obstacle," Novikov explained. "But if it works, it might be faster."

Konstantin looked at Praskovya. The security chief shrugged.

"It is worth a try," he said.

"Good," Konstantin said, turning back to Novikov. "Then get to it."

He left the room, slamming the door behind him, leaving the security chief and the operations director looking at each other through the swirling gray cloud of cigarette smoke.

Chapter 23

How?" Gates asked. "How are you planning to destroy the Vilanovsky?"

"That, commander, is my mission," McCabe said. "It's not your worry."

"Understood," Gates said. "But here's how I see it. You're not parachuting onto the platform, and you're not fast-roping either. Both require violating Russian airspace, and you'd be spotted by their air defense systems. Assault boats are no help. You saw how easily we spotted the Russians because of the midnight sun.

"That leaves a subsurface approach. It wouldn't be the first time the U.S. sent a sub into Russian territory. But I think in this case, our government would rather not violate Russian waters, not after the experience Sarah and I had. That leaves combat swimmers. Too far and too cold to swim to the platform, so that makes me think you'll be using a SEAL Delivery Vehicle. Still a frigid ride."

McCabe scratched his ear as a smug smile curled his lips.

"Your intel is dated, commander," he said. "We now use the new Dry Combat Submersible. Fully enclosed. It keeps us dry and warm."

Gates ignored McCabe.

"You can't place explosives at the base of the caisson," Gates said. "It's too thick, too sturdy. You'll have to place them above the caisson, on the outside decks. That means scaling the caisson walls. Difficult but not impossible. Except you won't have the element of surprise. When the Russians came after us, we turned off our deck lights to give *us* the element of surprise. But the Vilanovsky is covered with deck lights, and they have a well-armed security force. We only had fire hoses. The Vilanovsky has a water cannon on each corner of its first deck, and who knows what else."

McCabe sighed again.

"With due respect, commander," he said, "we've been planning this mission for weeks—"

"I'm sure of that, lieutenant," Gates interrupted. "But you weren't able to do an onsite reconnaissance of the platform. I've been there—twice. And my advice—speaking as someone with training in marine architecture—is the best way to bring down the Vilanovsky is not from the outside, but from the inside."

"I don't understand, sir."

"The Vilanovsky has an underwater portal into the caisson and a large moon pool."

McCabe stared at Gates for several moments before he said, "A portal? You mean a doorway?"

"An opening," Gates said. "We saw it before we were ambushed. It's how their DSVs and divers get access to the open sea."

"And you can tell me how to find it?"

"Better yet," Gates said. "I—and Sarah—can show you." He glanced at Sandford and Gunnar. "That is, if Sarah and Captain Gunnar agree."

Gunnar looked at Gates, then Sandford, then shook his head.

"After the last time, Doug, I don't think—"

He stopped when Sarah touched his arm.

"Please, captain." She pleaded with her eyes as much as her words. "For Johnny?"

Gunnar grimaced, shaking his head. Then, accepting defeat, he sighed, "Very well." He wagged his finger at Gates. "But you take care of her, Doug. And no more self-flagellation like last time if things get mucked up."

Gates smiled. "Yes, sir." He turned to McCabe. The frost in the SEAL's eyes melted the smile.

"I haven't agreed to any of this, commander," the SEAL said.

"Lieutenant, Sarah and I can get you to the rig, and we can guide your people inside fast. In and out, that's how you like it, right? And if everything goes to hell . . ." He nodded toward Sandford. ". . . We'll have the best damn submarine driver the Navy ever trained."

McCabe stared at Sarah. "Navy?"

Sarah planted her elbows on the table, rested her chin on knitted fingers, and batted her eyelashes at the SEAL.

McCabe ran his hands through his short blond hair, exhaling sharply. He paced back and forth in the conference room, then stopped in front of Gates. He held up an index finger.

"One, I can't make this decision on my own. I need to talk to my superiors," he said. Another finger joined the first. "Two, if they do approve, you two . . ." He waved indicating Gates and Sandford. "Do not leave your mini-sub. You guide us in, then you get the hell out of Dodge. Understood?"

Gates held up both hands in supplication.

"Understood, lieutenant."

"Fine." McCabe said, as he stomped out the door. "I need to make a call."

Gates smiled as he turned to Sandford.

"Sarah, you better go over Chip and make sure he's fit to sortie. Senior chief, help her with anything she needs." Leland caught Gate's eye. The dark eyes behind the black horn-rimmed glassed implored him. "Fine. You, too, Leland."

☼

Several miles to the north of the Franklin, an American special operations submarine nosed its way beneath the surface of the Arctic Ocean. Lieutenant Davids, second in command of McCabe's SEAL unit, stomped through the passageway, a message flimsy crushed in his hand. At his team's compartment, he stopped and gave three smart raps on the watertight door. There was a clunk as the dogging latches released and the door cracked opened. An unfriendly blue eye peered out at him.

"Open up, chief," Davids said.

The door swung open and Davids stepped into the compartment. Chief Drummond, the unit's senior noncommissioned officer, was short and stocky but well-muscled. Closely cropped light-brown hair crowned his head. One glance at Davids and he knew there was a problem.

"Bad news, sir?"

"Bad news, chief."

The converted ballistic submarine had a special compartment reserved for SEAL detachments. A row of bunks two high lined each bulkhead, leaving little room in between. As cramped as it was, it was a luxury compared to smaller attack subs. SEALs sat on the bunks. A few read books or magazines. Others cleaned weapons or sharpened knives.

A card table stood at the far end of the bunks, holding a scale model of the Vilanovsky. Davids, a tall, lanky officer in his late twenties, marched the length of the compartment until he stood next to the model.

"Listen up," he said. The sailors stopped what they were doing and turned their attention to him. "I just got message traffic from the skipper." He showed them the message flimsy. "The sub had to nearly surface to put its antenna up to download the message, so you know it's important. We've got new orders."

"Is the mission off, XO?" asked a commando, using the short-hand term for executive officer, or the next senior most officer of a team.

"No," Davids said, "but we're scrapping the plan we've spent the last several weeks on. Instead of assaulting from the outside—" Davids grabbed the top of the oil platform model and removed it from its base. He pointed to the interior of caisson. "—we're assaulting from within the caisson."

"How the hell are we supposed to get inside the caisson, XO?" Drummond said, his voice doubtful.

"Lieutenant McCabe says there is a portal into the caisson, chief," he said.

"A what?" a sailor asked.

"A door," Davids said. "An underwater entryway. We'll sail right through it."

"And then what, sir?"

"We'll blow the fucker up from the inside." Davids pointed to the inside of the model. "There's a moon pool here. We surface inside the rig, plant our explosives, and go out the same way.

"How does the skipper know about this portal, sir?" Drummond asked. "And the moon pool?"

"That Coast Guard team on board that research ship sent people over to the Vilanovsky. They got a good look at the moon pool and the rest of the rig. The ship has a DSV and a hotshot former Navy submersible pilot. The DSV pilot and a Coastie made an underwater recce of the rig. They found the entry." He hesitated before continuing. "They'll guide us in."

"For Christ's sake, the Coast Guard?" the chief growled. Grumbling echoed the chief's sentiment.

"Enough. Enough," Davids said, the message flimsy flapping in his hand as he tried to wave the compartment quiet. "They're only guiding us in, then they leave. We surface, get out of the DCS, set our explosives, and leave the way we came. It's an easier plan."

"Ours is not to reason why . . ." someone said, in a mocking voice.

"All right. All right," Davids said. "We've got a lot of planning to do. Chief, let's look at our intel on the Vilanovsky. Especially those news videos of its sister platform. Maybe there are interior images that might help."

"Yes, sir."

"What was that stuff about 'reasoning why'?" someone asked.

"It's from a poem," another answered. "'Ours is not to reason why, ours is but to do or die.'"

"We're fucked," someone else said.

Chapter 24

The deck was shaking again.

Konstantin watched the roiling surface of the coffee in his cup. Since the first sea quake two days before, the Vilanovsky's decks had rattled with growing frequency and strength. None of the scientists aboard the platform could offer an explanation other than the ocean floor in the Chukchi Sea was more seismically active than believed. The frequent shaking was adding to the equipment problems. Konstantin cursed. Too many delays. He was sick of so many delays.

"Excuse me, sir."

Novikov stood at the door of Konstantin's private quarters, a small suite that included a sitting room with a desk, a private toilet, and a small bedroom. It was modest by most standards, but compared to Novikov's one-room compartment, it was spacious.

Konstantin looked up from his coffee cup. Novikov appeared less nervous than usual.

"Good news, I hope," Konstantin said.

"Yes, sir," Novikov said. "I think so."

"You think so?"

"I think you will appreciate it," the ops director said.

"Then tell me," Konstantin growled. "Don't allow me to die in suspense."

"I am happy to report we positioned the lifting cradle over the obstacle and moved it out of the way of our target."

Novikov waited for Konstantin's congratulations. It never came.

"Why did it take so long?"

Novikov's face dropped. "I—I'm sorry, sir," he said. "But these sea quakes are creating even more problems with our equipment, particularly our electronics. We could not reposition the cradle automatically. We had to do so manually, with divers directing us from below. It was a very complicated procedure, sir."

"I am certain it was," Konstantin said, his tone not agreeing with his words. "When can we raise the object?"

"We are preparing to reposition the cradle now," Novikov said. "But again, we must do so without automation. It takes time."

"Time is something we are running out of, Sergey," Konstantin said.

The deck shook again, this time with more force. Konstantin's coffee splashed out of its cup. He grabbed at it, but the cup toppled onto its side. He looked up and saw Novikov supporting himself against the wall. The trembling subsided.

"Please carry on," Konstantin said. "And please hurry, before these cursed quakes bring the Vilanovsky down on our heads."

For the people attempting to raise the object below, the sea quakes were creating even more problems. The quakes were coming more frequently, almost as though on a schedule. The control room, perched atop the module containing living quarters, labs, and offices, swayed more from the quakes than the rest of the platform, interfering with the

165

Vilanovsky's electronic controls. On the moon-pool deck, the workers struggled to prevent the hydraulic lifting apparatus from swinging off its tracks. In the caisson below them, the quake-agitated water tossed the DSVs and hardsuit divers about like toys in a child's bath.

"The divers are getting tired, Novikov," Praskovya said in a soft but strained voice. "And so am I. How much longer do you think?"

Novikov held onto a control panel as another trembler rattled through the platform.

"You are tired?" he snapped. "We are all tired."

Through his weariness, the operations director remembered with whom he was talking and apologized.

"It is these quakes," he said in a gentler voice. "They not only slow the work, they make it impossible to sleep when one has the chance."

Praskovya waved off Novikov's concern, crimped the end of a Belomorkanal, and lit it.

"I understand, my friend," he said, though he didn't consider Novikov a friend nor even a colleague. "I misspoke myself. But our divers are reaching their maximum underwater time. We cannot afford to lose any more divers."

Novikov nodded. His heavy glasses slid down his nose. He pushed them back with a finger.

"Mr. Konstantin is insistent we speed up the work," he said. "He does not welcome my explanations. He is your friend, Praskovya. You can talk with him?"

Praskovya exhaled heavily, the smoke billowing through the control room. He nodded. "Perhaps I can speak reason with him."

Novikov watched the security chief leave. He didn't care for Praskovya. He had a good idea of the man's history and knew Praskovya had no high opinion of the scientists and technicians on the Vilanovsky, including himself. Even so, Novikov said a small prayer in his head that Praskovya would be successful in his mission.

Praskovya found Konstantin in his suite.

"What is it, Petya?" Konstantin said as Praskovya entered.

"The divers are nearing the safety limit for their time underwater," he said, deciding not to sugar coat his report. "They must surface and rest."

"Do we not have another shift of divers?" Konstantin demanded.

"They are on their rest period," Praskovya said.

"What about the third—"

"There is no third shift," Praskovya said. "We lost divers in the ambush on the Franklin's DSV and in the second attack on the Franklin itself. We only have enough men now for two shifts. They both are spent."

"*Proklyat'ye*!" Konstantin hammered the desk with his fist. "Goddamn it! I am sick of these delays, Petya!"

"I know. I know." Praskovya extended a palm to calm Konstantin. He tried to say something more comforting, but another tremor shook the room.

"And these damn sea quakes!" Konstantin said. "*Trakhayte ikh!* Fuck them!"

"In all the years we have worked together, Aleks," Praskovya said, "I have never heard you curse so much."

Konstantin rubbed his eyes with the heel of his hands, then did the same to his entire face.

"Yes," he sighed. "These damn temblors are stretching my nerves to the breaking point. At any minute, I feel this whole platform could pitch into the sea."

"That, my friend, will not happen." A new cloud of smoke circled Praskovya's head as he lit another cigarette. "The Vilanovsky is too sturdy for that to occur."

Konstantin launched from his chair, causing his chair to bang into the bulkhead. He walked around his desk, running both hands through his hair.

"And these constant delays. One after the other— equipment failures, the removal of the obstacle, and that cursed research ship." His arm flew out toward the Franklin. "And who knows what the Americans are planning to do?"

"Calm yourself, Aleks. Calm yourself." Praskovya stood, stepped to a cabinet where he found a bottle of vodka. He poured two stiff drinks and handed one to Konstantin. "What can the Americans do? Start a war over a simple oil drilling platform?" He grinned at Konstantin, the cigarette clenched in his teeth. "If they have not done so after the other night's operation, they are not going to do so. They are merely curious about our operations."

"What if they discovered what we are sitting on?"

"They cannot." Praskovya shrugged. "Though most likely they suspect." He paused, then shrugged again. "Perhaps *wonder* is a better word. Since what happened in 1968 to the K-129 and the others, every country with a navy and submarines recognizes these unknown subsurface phenomena exist. But the Americans have no way of knowing the Vilanovsky is anything more than an Arctic oil drilling platform."

Praskovya patted Konstantin's shoulder, then led him back to his chair.

"So, calm yourself, Aleks," he said. "We will let the divers rest. When they recover, we will complete repositioning the lifting cradle around the object and raise it into the moon pool."

Praskovya made a grasping motion with his hand, then raised his arm above his head.

"See?"

Konstantin smiled and shook his head.

"Very well, Petya," he said. "Rest your divers. How long will you need?"

"Forty-eight hours," Praskovya answered.

"Forty-eight!" Konstantin was on his feet again, shaking his head. "No. No. No. That is too long. Twelve. Twelve hours is enough."

Praskovya hushed Konstantin with a raised hand.

"If you kill my remaining divers," he said, "you will never get that object on board."

Konstantin dropped back into his chair with an angry sigh. "Fine. Forty-eight hours."

"Thank you, my friend."

As Praskovya left the suite, another trembler rattled the Vilanovsky. From inside the suite, he heard Konstantin's voice.

"Proklyat'ye!"

Chapter 25

Ready to return the favor?"

McCabe looked at Gates, puzzled.

"Favor?"

"To the Russians," Gates said.

"Oh," McCabe snickered. "Yeah, let's hope we have better luck than they did."

The sun had reached its midnight nadir and was inching back into a gray, overcast sky. What light it provided cast dark shadows among the chunks of drift ice. Gates stared at the Vilanovsky, a star burning on the surface of the ocean, and muttered something his mother used to say, "From your lips to God's ear."

Gates wore his full battle gear except his Kevlar helmet, which he held in one hand. In the other hand, he carried a borrowed M-4. McCabe eyed the weapon.

"You remember our agreement, commander?" the SEAL said. "You deliver us, then you're gone."

"Just for an emergency," Gates said with a shrug. "Semper Paratus. Always Ready. That's our motto, you know."

Gates climbed onto the DSV and offered McCabe a hand.

McCabe rolled his eyes. "Yeah, right," he said, and he grabbed Gates' hand.

He was no longer wearing his uniform. Instead, he wore plain black fatigues with no name or service patches and no rank insignia, with matching body armor and K-pot. He carried a Russian-designed AK-47, and a sidearm Gates didn't recognize.

Sterile, Gates thought. If the SEAL was killed or captured, nothing would link him to the United States. Plausible deniability.

Sarah Sandford was inside the DSV, prepping it for the sortie. The hum and whirl of electronics powering up flowed through Chip's opened hatch. Gates lowered himself through the scuttle, waited for McCabe to pass his gear through the hatch, then seated himself next to Sandford. McCabe came through the hatch and laid himself on the padded bench between the two pilot chairs.

Gerry Salcedo worked the controls of the A-frame again. The DSV shuddered, rocked, and lifted free of its railroad-car cradle. Salcedo waited until the DSV's swinging motion abated, moved it over the dark water, and laid it into the swells. The support RHIB came alongside and two divers climbed aboard to detach the lifting cables. One closed the hatch and tapped it twice with the butt of his dive knife before returning to the RHIB.

"Commander, dog the hatch, please," Sarah said. As Gates sealed the hatch, Sandford maneuvered the little submersible until it pointed on a direct course toward the Vilanovsky. "I'll run on the surface until the GPS tells me we're at the maritime boundary. Since we can't use our sonar, I want to maintain a visual lock on the platform as long as possible. Once I pull the plug, the IGS—inertial guidance system—will take over."

They rode in silence, the hum of the electric motors and thump of ice against the hull the only sound in the tiny compartment. When they reached the border, the GPS chirped.

"Okay, gentlemen," Sandford said, "here we go."

The DSV slipped into the depths. The water was near black. Inside Chip, the only illumination came from the control panels. Sandford pressed buttons on the display screen and sat back.

"Autopilot's driving us now," she said. "But keep a sharp lookout. If you see an uncharted undersea mountain coming at us, please let me know."

"How long?" asked McCabe.

"About forty-five minutes," Sarah said. "I've programmed the inertial guidance to warn me when we get within two miles of the Vilanovsky."

McCabe eyed his watch and nodded with approval. "So, you learned to drive these things in the Navy?" he asked.

Sandford nodded.

"How long were you in?"

"Twelve years."

"That's a long time," he said. "Why not finish your twenty and retire?"

"Learned I could make more money doing this as a civilian than as an enlisted woman," Sarah said.

"Huh," McCabe said. He glanced at Gates, who shrugged.

Sandford caught the glances and shook her head.

"Fucking lifers," she muttered.

They fell quiet again, the whirl of the electric impellers and the gurgle of water slipping past the hull the only noise. Out of habit, McCabe examined his AK-47.

"Please be careful with that thing," Sarah said, with a rough imitation of the actor Sean Connery. "Some things in here don't react well with bullets."

Gates and McCabe looked at Sarah, and she looked back at them with a straight face. The three of them laughed.

A buzz from the IGS told Sandford they were two miles from the Vilanovsky, and she resumed manual control of Chip.

"What do you want me to do, lieutenant?" she asked.

"Maneuver to within one thousand yards of the rig, and settle her on the sea floor," McCabe said.

"Him," Sarah corrected.

"Excuse me?"

"Chip is a he, not a she."

"Fine," McCabe said. "Lay him a thousand yards from the rig, then wait for my team to arrive and signal us." He glanced again at Gates, muttering, "No wonder she left the Navy."

"I heard that," Sandford said.

A few minutes later, Chip was sitting on the ocean floor. Outside the bubble cockpit, the sea was dark. An occasional fish, illuminated by the light from the control panel, bumped into the Plexiglas.

"Doug, how do we know there won't be divers or DSVs out here waiting for us again?" Sandford asked, her eyes straining to see beyond the confines of the bubble.

Gates' own eyes scanned the depths through a side window. "They detected us before because we were using sonar. I don't think they can hear us approach without it. But keep your eyeballs peeled."

"Eyeballs peeled, aye," Sarah said.

Minutes passed before McCabe pointed through the Plexiglas and said, "There!"

A dull light flashed in the distance, two flashes, and a pause. Two more flashes, another pause, then a final flash.

"That's the DCS," McCabe said. "That's my team."

McCabe drew a small, powerful flashlight from his armored vest, placed its lens against the Plexiglas and flashed it three times, paused, and flashed it once more. Three return flashes came from the DCS.

"Okay," McCabe said, "let's take her—him—in."

Sandford didn't move. Her face was drawn and tight, her full lips pressed into a thin line.

"Sarah?" Gates said. "Sarah, what's wrong."

"I don't know which way to go," she said. "It's so damn dark, I can't get my bearings."

McCabe glared at Gates. "I thought you said she could guide us in, commander," he said. "Well?"

"We first spotted the opening on the sonar," Sandford said. "When we got closer, we saw the glow of underwater work lights inside the caisson. But I'm not seeing any lights now."

"Maybe they took the night off," said Gates.

"Jesus," McCabe cursed and dropped his head onto his arms. "Just great."

"Shut up, lieutenant," Gates said. "Sarah, nose it ahead until the inertial guidance shows you're a hundred yards from the rig. Then turn on your flood lights. If anyone sees them, it'll be too late for them to respond before we get inside. That okay with you, McCabe?"

The SEAL thought it over and nodded.

"Yeah," he said, irritably. "Yeah, let's do it. Go, go."

Chip shuttered as it lifted off the sea floor. Sandford nosed it forward, fearful of hitting an unseen object. To starboard, Gates' eyes sensed a denser shade of black in the ocean.

"I think that's your DCS," Gates said. "Zero one five degrees."

"I don't see it," Sarah replied.

"I see nothing," McCabe said. "You sure?"

"I am now," Gates said, his voice rising. "Still fifteen degrees off the starboard bow and closing. Damn it, we're on a collision course!"

The dark cigar shape of the DCS loomed to starboard. Sarah responded without thinking, sending Chip straight up and to port. The g-force from the maneuver pressed Gates deeper into his chair. McCabe's Russian rifle fell from the bench seat and clattered to the deck. Through the bottom of the bubble canopy, Gates saw the black upper hull of the SEAL submersible as it passed inches beneath them.

"Oh, god. Oh, god. Oh, goddamn," Sarah chanted as she returned Chip to the proper course. "Oh, goddamn."

McCabe released a long-held breath. Gates freed his death grip on the bulkhead. He relaxed, took a deep breath, and said, "Fuck it, Sarah. Turn on your damn lights."

"Yes, Sarah, turn on your damn lights," McCabe repeated.

"Yes, oh, yes," Sarah said, and with a flick of her finger, the ocean lit up.

The lights showed they were less than three hundred feet from the Vilanovsky, the caisson towering above them. At the foot of the caisson, lay dozens of large boulders placed there to act as rip-rap to prevent soil erosion around the base of the rig. Off their port bow, only twenty yards away, stood the opening, a dark cave in the side of a man-made mountain.

"Nice navigating, Miss Sandford," McCabe said. He arched around and spotted the DCS behind them, showing a single, yellow light. "Take us in."

Chip closed to within several feet of the caisson, turned to port, and inched toward the opening. There was still no light emitting from the portal.

"Damn. It looks like they really *did* take the night off," murmured Gates.

"Fine with me," said McCabe.

The submersible reached the entry and entered. They were inside the caisson. Above them was the moon pool. A faint glow from the drilling deck lights filtered down.

Chip's floodlights illuminated something to starboard. As the lights moved across more of its surface, details became clearer. It was dark gray, almost black. The shark-like shape and the streamlined sail fin on top were unmistakable.

A submarine.

Chapter 26

Everything aft of the conning tower was missing. But with its sleek forward hull and the streamlined sail with its enclosed flak turrets there was no mistaking this vessel. This was the first submarine designed to live beneath the waves for days, even weeks. Faster submerged than surfaced, it set the standard for submarine design well into the early years of the Cold War.

"Is that—?" Sarah didn't finish her question.

"Yes," Gates said. "A Type XXI Walter U-boat."

Chip's flood lights drifted over the dead submarine, its hull unencumbered with sea growth and remarkably free of corrosion or rust, both due to the frigid waters. If not for the missing stern, the U-boat looked ready to surface and return to port.

"So, they did deploy one with the Walter engine," Gates muttered. "And they sent it after the Fast Movers. That's why they had a secret base in Russia."

"Appears it met the same fate as the K-129," McCabe said. "And the others."

"What happened to its stern section?" Sarah wondered.

"My guess is it blocked access to the Fast Mover, and the Russians started dismantling it piece by piece," Gates said. "After a while, they just dragged it way. You can see drag marks on the seafloor."

Gates pointed to where Chip's floodlights illuminated a deep gash gouged into the seabed.

"Jesus, how did they do that?" Sarah asked.

"Look up," Gates said.

Above the U-boat carcass loomed the menacing dark shape of a massive steel claw, its twin pincers agape, as if ready to grasp the derelict sub.

"My god," muttered Sandford.

"A lifting cradle," said McCabe. "Like we used in Project Azorian."

"I think if we follow those drag marks, we'll come to the Fast Mover," Gates said.

McCabe nodded his agreement, and Sarah turned Chip to port and followed the scored soil. Seconds later, her display console flickered and went blank. Sarah let out a small yelp as the submersible trembled and bucked like a plane trapped in turbulence. A moment later, the mini-sub settled and the display screen powered up again.

"What the hell happened?" demanded McCabe.

"I-I don't know," Sandford said.

"Gremlins," Gates said. "The Russians complained about gremlins affecting their equipment. Could it have something to do with the Fast Mover?"

McCabe shrugged. "Hell, if I know."

"If this . . . thing," Sarah said, "has an electrical discharge as Lieutenant Strange speculated, that might affect my controls—like an electromagnetic pulse. But what caused that turbulence?"

No one answered her.

At that moment, the DSV's floodlights fell onto a massive shape looming out of the darkness. Sandford reversed Chip's propellers to avoid colliding with it, causing the SEAL's DCV behind them to shoot past. The pilot of the SEAL vehicle reversed his propeller and swung to starboard to avoid hitting it.

"My god," Sarah whispered, awed. "It's huge."

McCabe nodded as if in a trance. "It's bigger than I expected," he said. "A lot bigger."

Sitting on the ocean floor, the object rose another twenty or thirty feet above them. Its surface—or was it skin? —was a mottled gray-brown. It appeared as long as the Nazi sub would be if it were still intact but shaped unlike any sub the three of them had ever seen. From a thick, contoured middle, the front, back, and sides tapered to a knife edge. The bow, or what Gates and the others judged to be the bow, came to a rounded tip, the sides sweeping back from there at a 45-degree angle, then rounding off again to meet in the back. The shape reminded Gates of the stingrays he had seen while diving on wrecks, but this ray—if that was what it was—had no stinger tail. There were no windows, no sign of a command bridge, no visible control surfaces. The stern showed no source of propulsion, propellers, or ducted impulse jets. Again, the image of a string ray came to Gates' mind as he remembered how the creatures flew through the water with graceful movements of their wing-like fins.

"Is it a machine or is it . . . alive?" asked Sandford.

"I'm not sure," Gates said. "The surface doesn't look like metal or flesh."

"Modern submarines have anechoic coatings on their hulls to reduce their sonar signature," Sarah said. "Maybe it's something similar?"

Something made Gates think otherwise. The object pulled at him, drew him to it like the moth to the flame. Even more, he sensed it thinking.

Gates shivered and shook those thoughts from his head. He patted McCabe's shoulder, leaned to his ear, and whispered, "We got you here. Now it's time for you to go to work."

McCabe started, having been lost in his own bewildering thoughts. He cleared his throat. "Yeah," he muttered, then tapped Sandford's shoulder, jerking her from her own musings.

"Take us up, Miss Sandford," he said, "if you please."

Chapter 27

When Chip broke the surface, Gates looked around the moon pool and became disoriented. Everything looked different than when he and Leland visited the Vilanovsky. Then the moon pool was only large enough to lower and retrieve submersibles and divers. Now it spanned most of the drilling deck.

"Jesus, this place is huge," McCabe said, staring out of the bubble canopy.

"It wasn't this big this when Leland and I visited," Gates said. "It was much smaller." He pointed to a corner of the caisson where removable deck gratings had been stacked in several neat rows. "They must be getting ready to lift that thing out of the water."

"We expected to have to neutralize workers," McCabe said, "but it's deserted."

"Good timing," Gates said.

McCabe pointed to a spot where a ladder led to the next deck. "Miss Sandford, if you could let me off over there, you both can be on your way."

"Aye," Sarah said, and maneuvered the DSV into position.

The SEAL DCV pulled up behind Chip. Its hatches opened and SEALs dressed in the same black fatigues as McCabe scrambled onto the drilling deck, broke into teams of two and, weapons at the ready, hurried to their assigned locations to plant their explosives.

McCabe stood and opened Chip's hatch. He hesitated, leaned back, and said, "Thanks for the ride."

"Good luck, lieutenant," Gates said.

"Thanks, commander."

McCabe started through the hatch but fell back into the cockpit as a wave smashed the DSV into the metal deck. Sandford's control panel flickered and died again as another wave slammed into Chip. Through the open hatch they heard the screech and grind of metal twisting and scraping against other metal. The deck grates heaved and threw the Navy commandos off their feet. They clawed at the grating to stop their slide into the icy moon pool.

The shaking subsided, the waves inside the moon pool settling into lapping ripples. McCabe climbed out, and Gates handed up his weapon and equipment. Gates raised his head out of the hatch and saw McCabe rushing toward his men. Behind Chip, the DCV was moving toward the center of the moon pool. Gates lowered the hatch, dogged it, then sat back next to Sarah.

"Let's get out of here," he said.

"My pleasure," Sandford said.

Sarah worked the controls, the propellers whined, but Chip didn't move. She tried again, but the submersible stayed put. She cursed.

"What's the matter?

"I'm not sure," she said. "I think that wave pushed our starboard impellers under the grating. We must be hung up on it. I can't shake us loose."

Gates grabbed his rifle, rose, and undogged the hatch.

"What are you doing?" Sarah demanded.

"I'm going to pry us loose," he said. He patted the M4. "Maybe I can get some leverage with this."

Gates found the starboard propellers' shrouds snagged beneath the grating. He positioned himself over the bow thruster, one foot on the grating, the other on the mini-sub and used his weight to push Chip lower in the water and away from the deck. The thruster slipped free. He repeated the process on the aft propeller.

It didn't move.

He tried again, placing most of his weight on Chip's hull.

Still nothing.

The Vilanovsky shook again. Gates jumped onto the undulating grating. Waves banged Chip against the decking again. Gates rushed forward and, using the rifle butt to fend off the DSV, kept the bow propeller from snagging again.

When the shaking stopped, Gates returned to the aft propeller, knelt, and peered through the metal weave of the grate. He took a flashlight from his ballistic vest and shined it beneath the edge of the deck grates. A large bolt protruding from the lip of the grating had hooked the thruster, penetrating its fiberglass shroud. Gates grabbed the M4, jammed its barrel between the grating and the shroud, and tried to lever the shroud loose. Still no movement.

Gates stood, placed one foot on the rifle's receiver, and laid his weight on it.

Crack!

With the shroud shattered, Chip floated free from the deck. Gates' M4—its barrel warped—slipped off Chip's hull and disappeared into the water.

Losing two rifles on the same mission, Gates thought. That will cost me dearly.

"Commander Gates?"

Gates jumped at the voice, spinning, and reaching for his Glock. He froze when he saw the diminutive figure of Nikki, the ship's steward, standing before him.

"Nikki, what are you doing here?"

"Captain Gunnar sent me to warn you," she said.

"Warn me? About what? How the hell did you get here?"

"Commander, you must warn the others." She grabbed the sleeve of his jacket. Her eyes implored him. "You must get them away from here."

"Why?" Gates demanded again. "What did Gunnar say? And why send you . . . and how?"

Nikki moved closer, standing on tiptoes so her large dark eyes peered straight into his.

"They are awakening," she said.

"Who?" Gates tried to pull away, but she was strong for her size and held him close.

"Those who sleep below," Nikki said. "They are awakening."

"I don't understand what you're saying, Nikki," Gates said, still unable to pull free from the girl.

"You see more than the others," she said. "You feel more than the others. Feel it now."

Gates' head spun. Images coursed through his mind. A dead submarine, but not the U-boat. A Russian sub. The K-129. A giant claw. A blinding flash and the claw, in tatters, sinking to the ocean floor, lying among the ruins of the crushed Russian submarine. A ship, the Glomar Explorer, bucking among massive waves, hull rupturing, water flooding in. The strange alien thing beneath the Vilanovsky, the sense he had that he could hear—no, feel it thinking. But now something else. An energy growing within it. A power building, waiting to be released—violently released.

He blinked. Nikki was still holding him, still staring. She let go of his jacket and stepped back.

"You know now," she said. It was not a question, but Gates nodded. "You must warn them."

Gates turned, spotted McCabe, and ran to him. He grabbed the SEALs by his harness.

"McCabe, you've got to get your men out of here," he yelled.

McCabe pulled himself loose and stepped back, his hand clenching the AK's pistol grip.

"What? What are you talking about, commander?"

Gates jabbed his arm at the moon pool.

"That thing down there," he said. "That Fast Mover. It's coming alive . . . waking up, whatever. When it does, it will release a massive jolt of energy. It will destroy this entire platform.

McCabe stared at Gates as if he were mad.

"I told you and that woman to get the hell out of here," he said. "I've got a mission."

"That thing's going to complete your mission for you," Gates said. "It's just like Project Azorian and the Glomar Explorer. Only there were thousands of feet of water between that Fast Mover and the Explorer. The ship was only damaged. This rig is sitting right on top of the Fast Mover down there. When it releases that energy surge, it will destroy the Vilanovsky."

McCabe started to speak, but another temblor struck, this one stronger than the others. It knocked both men to their knees. A section of girder from the overhead tore free with a terrible screech and tumbled into the moon pool, missing the SEAL submersible by only feet. The shaking tossed a SEAL from the bulkhead where he had climbed to place his explosive charge. McCabe and Gates, both still on their knees, watched other SEALs rush to the injured man's aid.

"It is happening now, McCabe," Gates said, low and slow. "We don't have much more time."

"How do you know, commander?" McCabe said. "Dammit, how the hell do you know this?"

Gates looked at the SEAL, realizing a truthful answer wasn't possible at this time. "I just know," he said.

McCabe glared at Gates, his lips a thin slit, his eyes probing the Coast Guard officer's eyes. He shook his head.

"It can't be," he muttered.

"It is," Gates replied.

"No, I mean you," the SEAL said. "I didn't believe them when they told me about you in my briefing."

Gates' breathing stopped for a moment.

"What about me?" he said, grinding each word he spoke.

"That you had some kind of psychic abilities," McCabe said. "That's why you got recruited for that team of yours."

Gates said nothing. He stared back at the SEAL's probing eyes. More shaking. Another overhead girder tore loose, landing only feet away from the two men. McCabe glanced at it, his face expressionless, lost in thought. He stood, followed by Gates. The SEAL pressed the push-to-talk button on his radio mic.

"McCabe to team," he said, slow and clear. "Abort. Abort. Abort. Everyone return to the DCV. I repeat, abort. Everyone return to the DCV.

McCabe waved at his men, counting them as they gathered and waited for their mini-sub. Then he looked back at Gates.

"I hope to god, you're right," he said. "Or I'll have one of the shortest Navy careers in history."

"I'm right," Gates said.

Gates spotted the stanchion Leland pointed out only a few days before, the one with a glass-enclosed button and the sign saying, in Russian, Emergency Alarm - Abandon Ship. Gates trotted over to it, smashed the glass with his ASP baton, and pressed the button.

A wailing shriek filled the drilling deck. Echoes of the alarm filtered from the upper decks. Gates walked back to McCabe.

"What the hell are you doing?" McCabe asked.

"My job," Gates said. "Saving lives. At least these people will have a chance to get to the lifeboats."

Chapter 28

The chilled Arctic air blew in through the conference room window, shattered only moments before by the violent bucking of the Vilanovsky. Konstantin and Praskovya, clinging to the large table to stay upright, watched as the pane bent, cracked, and burst. Konstantin cursed while the security chief watched, stoic and impassive, as shards of glass rained on them.

"They are getting worse," Praskovya observed. His words made wispy clouds of fog as he spoke.

When the rumbling eased, Konstantin leaped from his chair and took the phone from the bulkhead.

"Control, this Konstantin. A window has shattered in the conference room. Get a crew down here to board it up and clean the mess."

"As soon as we can, sir," said the control room technician. "We have reports of damage from around the rig. And our electronics here have gone out again. We are trying to reboot them now."

"Do what you can," Konstantin said. He hung up the phone and looked at Praskovya. "Their electronics are out again."

Konstantin paced the floor, shaking his head. "Damn those seismologists in Moscow. How do they expect us to complete this work if we cannot stay upright for longer than five minutes?"

"People are becoming afraid." Praskovya lit a cigarette. "They may panic."

Konstantin pounded one hand into the other.

"How much longer until we resume diving operations again?"

"We should begin in the morning," Praskovya said. "My divers will have had their required rest."

"Good, good," Konstantin said. "And until we can bring it on board?"

"Normally, we could raise it by late morning or early afternoon," Praskovya said. "Normally. But as you said, Aleks, we cannot stay upright longer than five minutes."

"That was an exaggeration," Konstantin said, waving the image away with a flick of his hand. "But your point is taken. How much longer with these interruptions?"

"Tomorrow, late afternoon or early evening," Praskovya said. "Assuming the lifting equipment isn't damaged by these seaquakes."

"Do it then," Konstantin ordered. He stepped back to the phone and lifted the receiver. "In the meantime, I will return to shore. I want to find two seismologists whose heads I can bang together." Into the handset, he said, "Control, Konstantin again. Alert my pilots. I will fly to the mainland at once."

As he replaced the receiver, the rig rattled again with such violence it threw Konstantin to the floor.

"Aleks!"

Praskovya stumbled toward Konstantin, again using the table to keep himself upright. Through the broken window, he heard the screech of tortured metal and the shrieks of workers. Konstantin was getting to his knees when Praskovya reached him.

"Correction," Konstantin said, "I will smash the heads of a dozen seismologists."

"Are you injured?" Praskovya said, helping Konstantin to his feet.

Konstantin touched his head and looked for blood on his fingers. There was none.

"No, except for a bump on the head," Konstantin said.

Then came the wail of the emergency klaxon.

"What the hell is that now?" Konstantin demanded.

"The abandon ship signal," Praskovya said. "Remember my warning that the workers may panic? I think they are. I will check on it."

Praskovya darted through the door, leaving Konstantin alone. Konstantin rubbed his head, looked around the room as if he could see the cacophony of the klaxons filling the room, and staggered toward the door.

"God dammit," he said. "Just get me off this accursed platform."

Praskovya waded through panicked workers jamming the passageway as they blundered their way to their assigned lifeboats. Burdened by thick, rubbery cold-water survival suits and life jackets, they reminded Praskovya of scared and confused penguins. He pushed through them without apologies. When he reached his office, Praskovya grabbed the phone and called the control center.

"This is Praskovya," he said. "Are your instruments working yet?"

"Yes, sir," was the reply. "They just came back on line."

"Where did the alarm originate?"

There was a pause as the control-room technician checked his panel. "From the drilling deck, sir."

"The drilling dec—" Praskovya's face drained of blood. "There is no one working on the drilling deck tonight, you fool."

"That's what the sensor is telling me, sir," the technician said. "There may be no one working the drilling deck, but that is where the alarm originated."

"Never mind that," Praskovya snapped. "Get on the address system and tell my men to arm themselves and report to the drilling level at once."

He slammed the phone down, took a ring of keys from his belt, and unlocked a drawer in his desk. From the drawer he took his sidearm and holster and strapped them to his waist as he crossed the room to a heavily built standing locker and, using another key from his ring, unlocked it. Inside was a row of MP5 machine pistols and, beneath them, loaded magazines and extra boxes of ammunition. Praskovya pulled out one of the MP5s, inserted a magazine, and worked the chamber. He grabbed two more magazines and pushed back into the swirling confusion of scared penguins.

The Vilanovsky had four large, high-capacity, self-righting lifeboats held in quick-launching gravity davits on each corner of the platform. The four lifeboats provided more than enough capacity to rescue everyone on board the rig. But panic bred from confusion and a failure to conduct regular abandon-ship drills left many of the workers milling around the corridors in tight knots, slowing Praskovya's progress as he clambered down one ladder after another toward the drilling deck. More than once he threatened to shoot people if they did not make way for him. By the time he traversed the maze of passageways and stairs, he was not only breathing hard but, despite the chill, sweating.

His guess—no, his fear—was the Americans had decided to . . . How did they say it? To turn the table. Yes, turn the table and assault the Vilanovsky. Perhaps the people in the Franklin's DSV had seen the underwater portal into the caisson before Praskovya's men attacked them. But why now? And with what force? Not with the handful of sailors—those Coastguardsmen—on the Franklin. And yet they did bloody Praskovya's own assault force. But, no. There must be American special operators involved—Navy commandos raiding from a nearby submarine. But why? Simple retaliation? An international tit-for-tat that could spur a war? That made no sense to Praskovya. What then?

Unless . . .

Unless the Americans knew what lay beneath the Vilanovsky.

But, how could they? Praskovya himself had supervised the erasure of the electronic recordings on the research ship. Were the rumors true the U.S. had a new spy ship disguised as a research vessel, a ship with a hidden trove of electronic sensors he and his men had missed?

When he reached the top of the stairs leading into the drilling deck, he knew his fear had come true. To his right, on the far side of the moon pool, was a small, cigar-shaped submersible. Several armed men in black uniforms were climbing into the mini-sub. Two of them were carrying a third, apparently injured man. In the middle of the pool, Praskovya saw the familiar yellow DSV from the Franklin.

So, the Americans did see the caisson portal.

To his left, he saw two more figures. One wore the same black fatigues as those boarding the black submersible, the other the familiar dark-blue fatigues of the U.S. Coast Guard. Praskovya recognized the tall American named Gates.

Why are they here? And why are they leaving? Why set off the emergency alarm?

Explosives.

The word screamed in his head. They came, placed charges, and were making their escape.

They must have sounded the alarm to minimize fatalities by giving people a chance to reach their lifeboats.

Admirable, Praskovya thought. Not something I would do, but admirable.

Praskovya glanced back at the crowded corridor behind him, hoping to see his men approaching. He saw only panicky penguins. If he waited for his men, the Americans would make good their escape. No, he must act now, to slow them until his security force arrived.

Praskovya jerked out the MP5's extendable stock, jammed it into his shoulder, and aimed at the two men below. He was halfway through his trigger squeeze when the next trembler struck.

Chapter 29

Gates didn't know how they ended up between the stacks of deck grates, whether it was survival instinct, training, or the heaving of the Vilanovsky itself. But as the first shots whipped past their heads, he and McCabe were already sprawled behind the cover provided by the steel decking. McCabe rebounded to one knee, raising his AK to return fire. Gates drew his Glock. The weapon felt small and impotent in his hand as he heard another round of automatic fire come from above them.

McCabe's rifle barked return fire. Gates poked his head above the piled grating and spotted Praskovya ducking back from the stairs as the SEAL's rounds pounded the landing.

"That's Praskovya," Gates said, "the Vilanovsky's security chief. There must be more behind him."

"Next time I fire, you get to your DSV and get the fuck out of here," McCabe said. "Understand?" Gates nodded. McCabe lifted his AK above the grates and shouted, "Go!"

Gates was three steps away from shelter when he realized McCabe wasn't firing. He turned and found McCabe struggling with his weapon's charging handle, trying to clear a jam. Another burst from Praskovya's MP5 and Gates leaped back behind the grates as ricocheting rounds sent a shower of sparks up from the steel deck where he had stood.

Praskovya's firing paused. When it started up again, the rounds were not coming in their direction. Small geysers spurted from the moon pool between Chip and the SEAL submersible. Sarah Sandford stood in the DSV's hatch staring at Gates, her face a mask of horror. He waved at her to close the hatch and leave.

"He's shooting at the subs," Gates said. "If he hits them, no one's going anywhere."

McCabe pressed his push-to-talk button. "Submerge and get out of here," he said. "That's an order."

Gates watched the two submersibles slip beneath the surface and disappear. McCabe cleared his jammed rifle and fired a burst up the stairs. Praskovya slipped out of sight again.

"Is there another way out of here?" McCabe asked.

"There's a door on the other side of these piles," Gates said. "It leads to the helo pad. Leland and I came in that way."

"Let's go."

"Then what?"

McCabe shrugged. "You any good at swimming?"

"I'd rather steal a lifeboat."

"That'll work," McCabe said. "Let's go."

They moved around the grating pile, Gates in the lead. Praskovya let loose another volley, the rounds pounding behind them. Gates heard his name called.

"Commander Gates!" Praskovya said. "That is you, isn't it, commander? How nice of you to visit us again. But I truly wished you had called first."

"Don't answer him," McCabe cautioned. "Acknowledge nothing."

The SEAL glanced at Gates' uniform. He drew a K-Bar knife from his belt and handed it to Gates.

"Here."

Gates looked at the knife.

"You want us to commit hari-kari?" he said.

"Your name and service tapes," McCabe said, not smiling. "Cut them off."

Gates pulled a folding knife from his vest and thumbed it open. McCabe sheathed his fighting knife and waited for Gates to cut off the embroidered name tape on the right side of his blouse, then the USCG tape on the left side. McCabe held out his hand.

"Your dog tags, too," McCabe said.

Gates snapped the chain holding his dog tags around his neck and handed them to the SEAL. He watched McCabe wrap the name tapes and dog tags up in the broken chain, then slipped the tiny bundle through the deck's steel lattice, letting it fall into the sea.

"Plausible deniability," Gates said flatly.

"Welcome to special ops," McCabe said. "Now the door."

☼

Praskovya glanced back at the corridor behind him, expecting his men to be thundering to his aid. It was empty. Even the clumsy penguins were gone. "*Chert voz'mi*," he cursed. "*Gde oni?*" Dammit. Where are they?

Praskovya stepped with caution from the door, eyed the drilling deck for the likeliest places to plant explosive charges, but saw nothing.

"Commander Gates," he called out. "It appears you missed your ride home. Why don't you come out and explain what you're doing here?"

Gates and McCabe eased around the corner of the piled grating they sheltered behind, keeping low and out of Praskovya's sight. There was a space between the stacks and the bulkhead, leaving enough room for a man to squeeze past. They slipped past two piles without problem. At the third, a length of grating jarred loose by the shaking, leaned at a precarious angle against the bulkhead. Gates crawled beneath it, followed by McCabe. As he rose on the far side, the SEAL bumped the grate. It teetered, then slid to the deck with an insidious screech. A burst from Praskovya's MP5 slammed into the piled gratings.

The shooting didn't move Gates. He stood transfixed, staring. McCabe moved to Gates' side and stared, too.

The last stack of grates laid toppled by the tremors, blocking the door. Both men cursed.

"Now what?" said McCabe.

Gates sat with his back against the bulkhead and said nothing.

McCabe sat beside Gates.

"How much ammo do you have?" he asked. He removed the magazine from his AK, checked it, then replaced it with a fresh one, and worked the charging handle.

"Three mags of fifteen rounds each, including the one that's loaded," Gates said. "You have a plan?"

"Basic tactics," McCabe said. "Attack into the ambush."

"You mean go out like Butch and Sundance."

"You have a better idea?"

Gates shook his head.

"Me neither," McCabe said.

Praskovya slipped further down the stairs, seeking an advantage point from which he could spot the Americans. He had a good idea what they were trying to do—reach the door leading to the helicopter pad. It was the only other exit and exactly what he would try. What they expected to do after that, he couldn't fathom. There was no other way off the Vilanovsky for them except the way they came aboard.

Half way down, he saw the toppled deck grates and smiled. *There is no escape for them now.* Nothing they could do but surrender. Or die. What would he do in their place? The answer was obvious. And just as obvious was what the Americans planned to do.

Praskovya crouched on the stairs, reducing his profile, shouldered the MP5, and aimed it at where he believed the Americans would rush from and waited.

Movement.

Just the tip of a gun barrel peaking around the second to the last pile of grates. He adjusted his aim and tightened his pull on the trigger.

From the pile came a shout. "Now!"

A burst of fire from an AK slammed into the landing well over Praskovya's head. A moment later, the two Americans rushed from their cover, spreading out left and right, increasing the tactical distance between them. Praskovya aimed at the man with the AK and pulled the trigger.

Then the Vilanovsky shook again.

Praskovya's burst went wide, but one round slammed into McCabe's leg. He fell to the deck, his momentum skidding him forward as he sprawled on his face. The AK flew from his grip, clattered across the grating, and disappeared into the pool. Gates saw the SEAL fall, spotted Praskovya on the stairs, and fired three times at the Russian. The shots missed, Gates' aim thrown off by the shaking. He watched

Praskovya turn the machine pistol toward him. A sick grin of satisfaction creased the Russian's face.

The shaking worsened. The section of deck plate Gates stood on heaved, lifting to a sharp angle. Gates jumped clear before the grate slid into the frigid moon pool. The screech of tortured metal pulled his attention back to Praskovya. The Russian still squatted in the middle of the stairs. The machine pistol was gone. His hands gripped the railing as the stairs swayed, strained, and broke free from the bulkhead. Suspended by a few remaining bolts, the stairs swung over the moon pool, paused, then dipped toward the water. Praskovya glanced at Gates, his face calm. Another metallic screech and an explosive crack as the stairs ripped free from their final bindings. They turned belly up, Praskovya still clutching to the railing, and collapsed into the water, dragging the trapped Russian into the depths of Chukchi Sea.

Chapter 30

G ates lurched toward McCabe. The SEAL fumbled with a combat tourniquet, trying to wrap it around his thigh, but the heaving of the deck and the pain from the wound thwarted his attempts. More metal tore loose from the bulkhead and the overhead. Gates sprawled across McCabe, protecting the SEAL's body with his own. Something the size of a hammer fell on Gates, striking the back plate of his armored vest. It felt like a punch to his kidneys.

Then the shaking stopped.

Gates took the tourniquet, wrapped it high on McCabe's thigh, ran the end through the buckle, cinched it tight, and tightened it further by turning the windlass. McCabe screamed as the band bit into skin and muscle, but the profuse bleeding eased to an ooze.

Gates grabbed McCabe's first aid kit and pulled out the combat pill pack, a small plastic bag containing oral antibiotics and a powerful non-opioid painkiller.

"I don't need that," McCabe said, pushing the proffered bag away. "We're both going to be dead in a matter of minutes."

Gates sat back, removed his Kevlar helmet, and ran his hand through his sweat-matted hair.

"I guess you're right," he said.

"Help me sit up," McCabe said.

McCabe gritted his teeth as Gates grabbed him beneath the arms and dragged him to where he could rest his back against the bulkhead.

"Thanks," McCabe said. "I'd hate to die on my back."

Gates looked at the SEAL, and the SEAL looked back at Gates. Both snickered.

"You know what I mean," McCabe said.

McCabe took off his own helmet and scratched his scalp.

"Sorry you got involved in this, commander," he said. "On the teams, we know there's always a chance we won't come back. That's part of our job, but it's not your job."

Gates recalled giving a similar speech only a couple of days before and snorted.

"There's an old saying in the Coast Guard, lieutenant," he said. "'You have to go out. You don't have to come back.'"

McCabe dipped his head and shook it. "Jesus, what kind of fools are we?"

"Poorly paid ones."

Bubbles in the moon pool caught Gates' attention. He tapped McCabe's shoulder and pointed.

"What's that?" he said.

A moment later, he had his answer as the black, rounded hull of the SEAL submersible broached the surface, followed by Chip's small yellow sail. Both vehicles eased up to the deck grates. The DCV hatch opened and two men emerged, rifles at the ready, scanning for threats. McCabe raised his hand in a weak wave. The two commandos waved back and picked their way through the debris.

Chip's hatch swung up, and Sarah Sandford leaned out of it. When she saw Gates, her eyes brightened and her smile broadened.

"Hey, sailor," she said.

Gates gave her a weak smile in return.

Lieutenant Davids, McCabe's team XO, and Chief Drummond knelt beside their leader and examined his wound.

"I ordered you to get the hell out of here," McCabe said.

"You'll just have to court martial me, skipper," Davids said.

"Really, sir, we didn't have a choice," Drummond added. "That crazy sub-driving lady blocked the exit with her submersible."

"We'll discuss this later," McCabe said. He grimaced as the two SEALs lifted him to a standing position. The SEAL leader stood on one leg, an arm around Davids' and Drummond's shoulders, as they linked hands to form a seat. They started back to the DCV, then stopped and turned.

"Hey, Coastie," McCabe said. "Thanks."

Gates nodded. "You, too, Squid," he said, using the nickname for Navy sailors.

The SEALs returned to their submersible, and Gates climbed aboard Chip. He settled into the second chair and looked at Sarah as she submerged the DSV.

"Did you really block the exit?" Gates asked.

She shook her head without looking at him.

"I was having mechanical problems." She gave him a sly smile. "That's my story and I'm sticking to it."

Gates grinned. "Let's get out of here."

As the DSV steered toward the portal, its floodlights illuminated the Fast Mover. It looked different. Its position had changed, turned to the right. Gates saw where the wings—he couldn't think of a better term—gouged the sea floor.

There was something else, though, a change in its color. Instead of mottled gray and black, it was luminescent. A series of images, shapes and shadows flashed through Gates' head, possibilities and improbabilities, so many, so fast, they remained indistinct, like a fading memory of a dream.

The object moved, a trembling that reminded Gates of a bear waking from its long winter slumber. Another more pronounced tremor and he gripped his seat.

"Hold on!"

Wave or pulse, it sent Chip careening through the portal. Ahead of them, the SEAL submersible struggled with its own mad yawing. Sarah cursed, struggling for control, willing with the strength of her concentration the DSV to answer its helm. When it did, Sarah sighed.

The SEAL vehicle turned to port, taking up a course returning them to their mother sub. Sarah set her course for the Franklin and settled back.

"What happened back there?" she asked. "To the guy shooting at you?"

"He's dead," Gates said.

"Did you—"

"No," Gates said. "The stairs collapsed under him and they both fell into the moon pool."

"So that's what that was," Sarah said. "Scared the bejesus out of me."

Gates stiffened in his seat. "Oh, my god. Nikki!"

"What?"

"Nikki, who came to warn me," he said. "Did she get off?"

"Who?" Sarah said.

"Nikki, the young girl who warned me the Fast Mover was waking up. Did she make it off the rig? Did you see her?"

"Doug, all I saw was you, McCabe, the SEALs, and that guy with the machine gun."

"We've got to go back."

"Are you crazy?"

Sandford never got her answer. A force stronger than the previous struck the DSV. It spun the submersible and pushed it through the sea like the hand of God.

The last thing Gates remembered was the sound of Sarah's screams.

Chapter 31

Konstantin stumbled and cursed. He was unaccustomed to carrying his own bags and the Vilanovsky's swaying, the bustle of the frightened rig crew trying to reach their lifeboats, and the constant whine of the emergency alarms, only exasperated his own clumsiness. This was not the orderly exit from the drilling rig he had planned when he first told his pilots he was leaving for the mainland. This was a panicky flight from an engineering miracle that was shaking itself apart.

He hadn't seen Praskovya since the security chief dashed from the conference room. He had no way of knowing where his old friend was. *Making his way toward a lifeboat like the others, no doubt.*

He wished Praskovya was with him at that moment. Throughout their many missions, when times were dire, the former commando's placid reserve had helped Konstantin stay calm. But here he was sweating heavily in the bitter air, his labored breathing pumping plumes of white condensate, and he could not deny he was panicking. He was afraid. No, he was terrified.

Despite the wail of the siren, he heard the whine of the Kamov Ka-62's twin turbojets starting. He followed the sound, elbowing through the crowd, stumbling on the trembling deck. Some fool pushed him, causing him to trip over one of his bags. For a moment he feared being trampled, but someone more level-headed helped him to his feet.

He looked for his bags. They were gone, carried along by the crowd. He dismissed the loss with a wave of his hands and plowed through the throng toward the helo pad. Somewhere along the way, he lost his fur cap. Ahead, the sound of the turbojets deepened as if the Kamov were lifting off. *Were the cowards leaving him behind?*

He reached the landing pad, and the Kamov was still there. Sukelov, the copilot, stood next to its small stairs, waiting for him.

"Mr. Konstantin, thank god," the copilot said. "Do you have luggage?"

"Never mind that," Konstantin growled as he climbed the stairs. "Let us get off this death trap."

Konstantin fell into a chair as Sukelov lifted the stairs inboard and secured the hatch. He secured his seatbelt as the turbojets screamed, the propellers overhead bit into the air, and the helicopter leaped from the platform.

As they gained altitude, the full damage from the quakes came into view. The once pristine Vilanovsky was a wreck, with equipment toppled and a section of one module's roof collapsed. Fires licked from beneath the wreckage, belching black smoke. Konstantin saw the lifeboats fall one by one from their davits, plunge into the sea bow first, disappear, then bob back to the surface like corks, and motor away from the rig as fast as they could.

The helicopter circled the scene at low altitude while the pilot radioed a distress message. Konstantin watched transfixed as the Vilanovsky gave a great shudder, and its towering drilling derrick swayed, bent, then tumbled to the deck. His hand ached, and he glanced at his bloodless fingers digging into the armrest of his chair.

All this work, he thought. All the years and the technical difficulties they overcame. The once-in-a-lifetime chance to discover and contain a new source of boundless energy. All lost. Lost because some scientist, some seismologist parading around as an expert, did not warn them the floor of the Chukchi Sea was seismically active. *For want of a nail, the war was lost.* When he arrived back in Moscow, he would make certain the head of that *Sukin sy*, that son of a whore, rolled.

The Vilanovsky heaved, rising straight out of the water, and collapsing back onto itself. The surrounding sea boiled, then erupted in a massive surge of energy that carried part of the ocean into the sky in an expanding wave. This was no ordinary seaquake, Konstantin thought. No quake could do that.

Konstantin saw a large glowing object rise from the Vilanovsky's grave. It raced away at an unbelievable speed just below the surface. Then Konstantin understood. No sea quake wreaked this destruction. What sat below the Vilanovsky did.

That object. That damned object.

The energy wave sped closer to the Kamov. Konstantin heard the pilot curse and Sukelov scream. The wave cracked the helicopter's fuselage like an egg shell. For a moment Konstantin was flying free, still strapped to his seat, tumbling through the air. And in that last second of consciousness, of life, he glimpsed in the distance the object as it skimmed beneath the waves deeper into the Arctic Ocean and the shelter of what remained of the thicker ice.

Chapter 32

I t was several hours before Gates regained consciousness. He woke in his own bed aboard the Franklin. Sarah Sandford, sitting in a chair at his bedside, greeted him with a kiss and a warm smile.

That fabulous smile.

The blow to the head he suffered as Chip tumbled out of control left Gates with a concussion. His head throbbed and his stomach heaved. He reached out to touch Sarah's face and felt the sudden need to race to the head. Frank Chee warned Sarah of the concussion's aftereffects, and she was ready with a waste can for Gates as he retched.

"So much for romantic reunions," Gates muttered.

"Here," Sarah said, handing him a glass of water and two pills when he finished. "Your medic said these should help your stomach and your head."

Gates took the pills, washed them down with the water, then leaned back on his pillow with a moan.

As he recovered in bed, Sarah and Leland Strange filled Gates in on the aftermath of the aborted Vilanovsky raid. Because of the turbulence experienced inside the moon pool, Sarah had strapped herself into her pilot's chair with the seat belt. She blamed herself for Gates injury; in the excitement of the escape, she forgot to warn him. The blast wave or energy wave or whatever the hell it was the Fast Mover created, hurled Chip forward as if it were a body surfing on an underwater wave. Once it dissipated, and

Sarah regained control of the DSV, she discovered they had covered more than half the distance to the Franklin. Chip was a wreck, with most of its impeller pods torn away. The main section of the DSV, designed to withstand the pressures of the ocean's depths, remained intact. The little sub limped back to its mother ship like a battle-scarred veteran.

There was less knowledge of the fate of the Vilanovsky. Moscow simply reported "a catastrophic mechanical failure" doomed the oil rig. The Kremlin also said since drilling operations had not started, there was no oil spill.

"Of course, we know the Vilanovsky wasn't built for oil drilling," Strange added.

According to Moscow's report, most of the Vilanovsky's crew got away in the rig's lifeboats and survived. However, Konstantin and his two pilots were missing, as was an unnamed chief of security. Rescue efforts were still ongoing and the United States joined with several other nations in offering to help with those efforts. Moscow had not responded to the offers.

"And the Fast Mover?" Gates asked.

Strange shrugged.

"Don't know, sir," he said. "My guess is it got away, same as the one the Glomar Explorer was after. Funny thing is, as soon as the Vilanovsky collapsed and, I assume, the Fast Mover escaped, our power came back online, including main propulsion. Captain Gunnar waved off the rescue tug and has the Franklin underway and headed toward Nome. Chief Stalk reports all the spy gadgets in the hidden compartment are up and running again, too. Just turned on by themselves, she said. You think that Fast Mover was affecting our power network?"

Gates winced as he nodded. "I think so. I think it—they—wanted us to stay."

"They?" Sarah said.

Strange leaned closer to Gates and whispered, "You talked to it, didn't you, sir?"

Gates gave the young officer a sharp look. He glanced at Sarah. She gave him an odd look.

"Sorry, sir," Strange mumbled, backing away.

"You *are* psychic," Sarah declared. "Just like—"

"Just like what?" Gates demanded.

"Well . . . Captain Gunnar hinted that . . ."

Gates sighed.

"It wasn't talking," he said. His eyes focused on something not in the cabin. "More like being shown . . . images of things I don't fully understand. But I got the impression it was 'they' and not 'it.'"

"But why would they want us to stay, sir?" Strange asked.

"To help them," Gates said. "And to warn us again to stay away from them."

Gates shut his eyes.

"Leland, I need to rest," he said. "I feel like shit."

"Sure, sir," Strange said. "Rest up."

He started toward the door, then stopped.

"Oh, one more thing, sir," he said. He waited until Gates opened his eyes again. "The admiral called on the sat phone. He said he received a message for you from Lieutenant McCabe. It was routed from the sub his team was on through SUBPACFLT to the admiral. Funny message. All it said was, 'Thanks again, Coastie.'"

Gates smiled and said, "Good. That means his team made it back okay."

Strange opened the door to leave, stepped aside as Captain Gunnar entered, then left

"How's our patient?" he asked Gates.

"I've felt better, captain," Gates said.

"I'm sure you have, Doug," Gunnar said.

He glanced at Sarah, and she mouthed, *He needs to sleep*. He nodded.

"Well, I just wanted to check in on you," Gunnar said. "I'll leave you in Sarah's capable care. Get some rest, son."

Gunnar turned to the door, but Gates called his name.

"Yes, Doug?"

"Captain, did Nikki make it back to the ship okay?"

"Who?"

"Nikki. She said you sent her to warn me."

"Warn you?" Gunnar said. He looked at Sarah. She shrugged. "Who are you talking about, Doug?"

"Nikki, the ship's steward," Gates said. He tried to raise himself. The pain in his head forced him back into his pillow. His eyes closed in concentration, trying to remember how to pronounce the girl's full name. "Panik Ublureak. A small, attractive Inuit girl."

Gunnar stared at Gates, then at Sarah. His lips pursed for a moment, then formed a small, wry smile. A glint shown in his old, sea-gray eyes.

"Doug, there is no steward on my crew," he said. "And no Inuit girl named Nikki."

Gates eyes flashed open and he stared at Gunnar.

"But—"

"You know, Doug, I started my sea-going career in these waters. Spent several years plying the trade in and around Alaska and Canada. Got to know many Inuits—even learned a little of their language. This name you gave me—Panik Ublureak—I recognize it from the Inuit mythology."

"Mythology?" Gates said.

"Many Inuit cultures believe their ancestors or their gods came down from the stars," Gunnar said.

"That's what Nikki said," Gates replied. "She told me her people originally came from the stars and settled here. She seemed . . . She seemed to have this amazing ability to predict when and where a meteor would fall from the sky."

Gunnar nodded, his eyes still twinkling.

"Perhaps, Doug, they weren't meteors," Gunnar said.

Gates studied the old seaman while he rubbed his aching head. "Captain, you're making my head hurt worse," he said. "If not meteors, what could . . ."

Gates' words trailed away. His mouth drooped open and his eyes widened. He looked back at Gunnar, shaking his head.

"No, couldn't be," he said. "Could it?"

"What?" Sarah looked at both men. "What?"

"What I'm saying, Doug, is this: strange and mysterious things happen at sea. You say you met a young steward on this ship when no such person exists. You saw her again on the Vilanovsky where she tried to warn you."

Gunnar opened the cabin door and smiled at Gates. His eyes shined with good humor.

"Doug," he said, "Panik Ublureak is Inuit for Daughter of the Stars."

Gunnar stepped through the door and closed it. Gates lowered his head back onto the pillow and groaned.

"Doug," Sarah said, "what did Gunnar mean by that?"

Gates squeezed her hand.

"Just as he said," Gates said. "Strange and mysterious things happen at sea."

Author's Note

This is a work of fiction. However, many of the incidents mentioned in this story actually occurred. In 1968, four submarines from different countries did disappear within weeks of each other. Wreckage of three of those subs have been located, including the Russian K-129 which the CIA tried to raise with the Glomar Explorer. The cause for the loss of those submarines has never been definitively determined. Operation Mainbrace was an actual NATO naval exercise. According to contemporary news reports, it was plagued with sightings of mysterious air and undersea craft. A secret German facility, described in local news accounts as a U-boat base, was discovered in northern Russia in the 1980s. What it was used for, no one knows, though the Germans did establish a number of secret weather stations throughout the Arctic during WWII, including in Allied territory. The stories of the Octavius and the Baychimo are true. In fact, Alaska's state government launched a search for the Baychimo, now presumed sunk as she has not been spotted since her last appearance in 1969. Submariners have repeatedly reported hearing strange and unidentifiable sounds while travelling beneath the Arctic ice. Altogether, this just proves that fact is, indeed, stranger than fiction.

About the Author

M artin Roy Hill is the author of the award-winning Linus Schag, NCIS, thrillers, the Peter Brandt thrillers, *Eden: A Sci-Fi Novella*, and the award-winning collection of short stories, *DUTY*. He is a former journalist and national award-winning investigative reporter for newspapers and magazines. His nonfiction work has appeared in *Reader's Digest*, *LIFE*, *Newsweek*, *Omni*, and many others. He has written articles on military history for several publications and websites. His short fiction has appeared in *Alfred Hitchcock Mystery Magazine*, *ALT HIST: The Journal of Historical Fiction and Alternate History*, *Nebula Rift*, *Mystery Weekly*, *Crimson Streets*, and others.

Martin served in the U.S. Coast Guard Reserve, the Navy Reserve, and the California National Guard. He lives in San Diego, California, with his wife, Winke, son, Brandon, and their feline overseer, Harry.

Follow Martin Roy Hill on Facebook at https://www.facebook.com/Martin.Roy.Hill, on Twitter at https://twitter.com/MartinRoyHill, or visit his website at https://www.martinroyhill.com.

If you enjoyed reading this book, please leave a review on Amazon.com, Barnes & Noble, Goodreads, or your favorite review site.